SECRET OF LOVE

GLENNA FINLEY

A SIGNET BOOK

NEW AMERICAN LIBRARY

PUBLISHER'S NOTE

This book is a work of fiction. Names, characters, places, and incidents either are the product of the author's imagination or are used fictitiously, and any resemblance to actual persons, living or dead, events, or locales is entirely coincidental.

NAL BOOKS ARE AVAILABLE AT QUANTITY DISCOUNTS WHEN USED TO PROMOTE PRODUCTS OR SERVICES. FOR INFORMATION PLEASE WRITE TO PREMIUM MARKETING DIVISION, NEW AMERICAN LIBRARY, 1633 BROADWAY, NEW YORK, NEW YORK 10019.

 SIGNET TRADEMARK REG. U.S. PAT. OFF. AND FOREIGN COUNTRIES
REGISTERED TRADEMARK—MARCA REGISTRADA
HECHO EN CHICAGO, U.S.A.

SIGNET, SIGNET CLASSIC, MENTOR, ONYX, PLUME, MERIDIAN and NAL BOOKS are published by NAL PENGUIN INC., 1633 Broadway, New York, New York 10019

First Printing, July, 1987

1 2 3 4 5 6 7 8 9

PRINTED IN THE UNITED STATES OF AMERICA

For my mother

Every secret a man tells to a woman
is a sticking-plaster that attaches him
to her, and often begets a second secret.

—JEAN PAUL RICHTER, 1795

1

Miranda Carey stifled a groan as she shifted her position, trying to get comfortable on the stone bench outside the arrivals terminal at the Munich airport. It wasn't an altogether successful maneuver because stone benches aren't noted for soft surfaces anywhere in the world. When coupled with a mid-day July temperature in the nineties, even a bed of nails atop one of Greenland's icy mountains sounded inviting.

Miranda wouldn't have been on the bench at all except that the only vacant seats inside the terminal were at the coffee bar and she'd already consumed three cups of espresso while waiting for Mitchell Emerson to arrive.

Most employers would have realized the draw-backs of such a meeting place, she thought irritably, moving toward the very end of her bench to stay in the only bit of shade. Practically any other man would have suggested a rendezvous at an air-conditioned hotel like the one she'd just checked out of in the center of town. Or, if not that, there was the obvious locale—aboard the new cruise ship, even then waiting at its Danube pier. All her new employer had to do was deliver her cruise tickets and then go about his business, whatever it was at the moment. Just because he was the publisher of a monthly cruise guide didn't mean that he had to personally check out each new employee.

Miranda chewed nervously on the edge of her lower lip, acknowledging silently that perhaps she might be doing Mr. Emerson a slight injustice. Probably he'd been told that this was her first salaried position— ignoring her two years of free-lance travel writing. It didn't help that Barry Perkins, who edited the cruise guide, was also Miranda's cousin. Unfortunately, nobody knew that Barry was so wary of nepotism that he wouldn't have given her the job if a tight deadline hadn't forced the issue.

"I'm not concerned about your turning in a satisfactory article on this job," he told her on the way to JFK. "Even so, it looks like the very devil hiring family. This isn't Hollywood, but dammit all, Mitch isn't in town so I can get his okay." Barry changed lanes abruptly as a car cut in front of them. "Sometimes I wish I had a bulldozer blade," he added bitterly, after a muttered expletive which couldn't have been printed in his magazine. Then, reverting to his former complaint, "I can imagine the tom-toms are beating all the way to the coast now about my hiring a cousin."

"That's ridiculous. You shouldn't take things so seriously."

He spared her a quick sideways glance. "I like to eat regularly. Why in the deuce couldn't you wear heavy tweeds and thick stockings?"

"In July? In this humidity?" Miranda sat forward in the car and pulled her sheer cotton blouse away from her shoulders. "Then they'd accuse you of hiring a mental case."

"That might be better than having to explain a

blue-eyed blond. Natural blond with all the right measurements," her cousin said, sounding aggrieved again. "Especially these days."

Miranda started to laugh helplessly, shaking her head.

He grinned then, but still sounded defensive as he said, "Do me a favor. At least try to appear business-like when you pick up the tickets from Mitch in Munich. You might screw your hair into a knot and wear a baggy skirt."

"That's businesslike?"

"Oh, hell! You know what I mean. It would help if you looked less dewy-eyed—"

"Now see here—I'm almost twenty-five and it's not dew," she said, blotting her face with the back of her hand, "it's perspiration."

"Don't change the subject," he countered. "I'm telling you that Mitch doesn't go for bright-eyed ingenue types when he's paying them a salary."

"I gather he feels differently in his private life."

"He hasn't asked my opinion. I learned long ago that editors only discuss things like deadlines and editorial policy with their bosses if they want to stay around long enough to collect the next paycheck. Besides, Mitch's private life is his business. That's one of the advantages of being a bachelor which still exists," her cousin added, sounding smug.

"I can't wait until you get your comeuppance," she told him. "One of these days, you'll fall in love and join the rest of the human race."

"How would you know? You haven't shown any great rush to join the 'forever-after' franchise." Barry braked slightly as they approached the freeway exit for the airport. "Now—do you have everything you need? Passport? Traveler's checks? Toothbrush?"

"You don't have to tie a note around my neck asking the stewardess to look after me," Miranda said, more resigned than annoyed. Barry was inclined to act like a Dutch uncle rather than a cousin, at the slightest provocation.

"Okay, then. How about luggage? Can you manage?"

"Strictly mobile. There are these things called wheels," she said, hiding a grin. "They came in when porters went out."

"You don't have to convince me. Save your efforts until you meet Mitch in Munich. I've made sure that you get a chance to do this article on the new Danube service, but after that, he may politely wave you on your way. At least you'll get a trip abroad and a cruise on the house."

"That's fair enough. I may even impress him enough that he'll offer me a five-year contract."

"Don't count on it," Barry said, pulling up in front of the departure sector for her airline. "I *definitely* wouldn't count on it. That's not magazine policy."

"Well, it was a nice thought," she said, opening the car door as he braked to a stop. "No, don't get out, I can manage okay," she added, reaching for her big bag and pulling a shoulder tote bag after it. She knelt on the seat to drop a hasty kiss on Barry's cheek. "Don't worry about the deadline on the Danube cruise—I'll get the article to you in plenty of time. And it'll be terrific—wait and see."

"I'm not worried." He gave her a wide grin. "Believe it or not, that's why I hired you. Have fun."

"I will." She stepped back to wave him on his way. "Thanks for the lift."

Miranda had done her best to put Barry's mild warning out of her mind, but even her stay in Munich hadn't done much to dull the overtones. "It's just jet lag," she muttered, mopping her perspiring forehead with the back of her hand because it was too much trouble to search through her bulging purse for a handkerchief. "If that idiot doesn't get here with the tickets pretty soon . . ."

"Miss Carey?"

The masculine voice behind her held enough authority that Miranda jumped at least an inch off the hard stone bench and managed to trip over her tote bag as she hastily got to her feet. "That's right," she said. "I mean—I'm Miranda Carey." As her glance swept the unsmiling countenance of the dark-haired man surveying her, she asked hesitantly. "Are you—"

"Mitch Emerson," he replied in a level tone. "The idiot with your tickets."

Miranda closed her eyes, hoping that when she opened them again she'd find the encounter was a fantasy; the consequence of staying out in the sun too long. She opened her eyes slowly and then shook her head. Her employer's expression had grown even more forbidding in the interval.

"Barry didn't tell me that—" Mitch Emerson broke off his accusation in mid-sentence as he saw her sway. He reached across to clutch her arm. "What's wrong?" he asked roughly, his rugged features softening for the first time.

"Not a thing," Miranda flared back, furious at her moment of weakness. She pulled away, trying to dislodge his grip. "It's just so hot."

"Then why in the hell are you waiting out here in the sun? There's a perfectly good air-conditioned lounge in there." With his free hand he gestured toward the terminal some twenty feet away.

"I didn't want any more coffee," she started to reply but hastily changed the subject as she saw his eyebrows go up. "It doesn't matter. Besides, I'm really all right."

He released her arm then, but his expression was still wary. "I'll take your word for it. In the meantime, humor me."

"What do you mean?"

He picked up her bags, lingering just long enough to say, "*I'd* like a cup of coffee and I prefer it accompanied by air conditioning. We'll have our discussion in the terminal."

Miranda trailed reluctantly behind his tall form toward the glass doors of the building. "I didn't know we were having a discussion."

Her muttered comment was evidently loud enough to reach Mitch because he announced, "Well, now you do," over his shoulder without bothering to look at her.

Miranda had an opportunity to size him up as he paused at the automatic doors to let her precede him into the big waiting room of the airport. Barry hadn't mentioned that the man was so good-looking or so tall, she thought as he led the way to the familiar environs of the coffee bar. The scorching temperatures apparently didn't bother him because he looked cool and comfortable in a short-sleeved gray sport shirt and cotton slacks. The outfit provided her with an excellent view of impressive shoulders and a trim waist. Obviously her employer worked at staying in shape. It was hard to guess his exact age—probably mid-thirties, she decided, and wished she'd thought to ask Barry. Certainly there wasn't any gray showing in his thick dark brown hair and his skin was firm over high cheekbones and a chin that looked as solid as Plymouth Rock.

"How long have you been out in that sun?"

Mitch's question brought Miranda out of her mental stupor. She glanced around to see he'd pulled up by two vacant stools at the coffee counter and was obviously waiting for her to get onto one.

"Twenty minutes or so," she countered. "Why?"

"I should think that was obvious," he said, gesturing impatiently toward the counter.

"I was just—thinking."

"Perhaps you could do it sitting down," he replied, his tone noncommittal.

Miranda considered telling him that she'd already consumed so much caffeine that she could float down the Danube unaided, but decided against it. Considering her jet lag, maybe extra coffee wouldn't matter.

"You're doing it again."

His tone was resigned, but it still had enough bite that Miranda lost no time in scrambling up onto the stool. "Sorry. I'll try to reform."

"Cappuccino?" Mitch asked, settling onto the stool beside her after stashing her big bag next to the post beside him and placing her tote on the floor between their stools. "Or would you prefer something cold?"

"Cappuccino will be fine," Miranda said, matching his businesslike approach. After a quick look at her watch, she added, "I'm supposed to catch the bus to Passau in a few minutes. It's the one that connects with the cruise ship."

"I know, I've already talked to the driver," he went on after taking time out to give their order. "You don't have to worry about missing the bus—it'll wait for you."

"You mean, it's already arrived?"

He nodded. "Out in the parking area. They announced it over the public-address system in here."

He didn't say anything about how it would have been more sensible for her to wait in a place where she could hear vital bits of information, but Miranda was sure that the thought had occurred to him. It was even more pronounced in her mind at his next comment.

"I wanted to check your qualifications before we part company. There were a few things that your cousin didn't mention."

It would have been much nicer if he'd said "my editor," Miranda decided, seething, but she kept her voice as bland as his. "I'm sure that it wasn't intentional on Barry's part. What do you want to know?"

"We can't settle it in the time we have left now," he replied, glancing at his own watch. "Is it too much to hope that you're carrying a résumé or some of your published pieces with you?"

"I'm afraid so." Miranda chewed uneasily on the edge of her lip again. "But Barry certainly looked them over."

"I have great faith in his editorial skills. However," he added before she could get her hopes up, "I make it a policy to check out these things myself."

Miranda was tempted to ask how far down the personnel ladder his scrutiny went, but the look on his face deterred her. He obviously wasn't ecstatic about the newest addition to his editorial staff. In fact, she would have bet her last traveler's check that, if given the opportunity, he would have sent her home with a polite, but very firm, dismissal. Her fears were confirmed when he said, "Exactly what kind of time limit did Barry mention on this job?"

Miranda kept her glance on her newly arrived cup of cappuccino rather than meeting his gaze. "He wasn't specific on that." As the silence lengthened, she went on defensively, "He was more interested in my obtaining details on the new ship and the attractions at the ports of call. You know—the usual things."

"*I* know," Mitch said, spooning sugar into his coffee. "But do you?"

"I *have* been free-lancing in the field for two years—"

"How old are you?" he cut in before she could finish.

"Twenty-five," she said, crossing her fingers out of sight. Then, when he didn't answer, she glanced sideways and met his skeptical look. "Almost twenty-five. Next month," she added firmly. "Barry also said the the magazine would take care of my round-trip transportation and a reasonable expense account. All I have to do is pick up the cruise tickets from you," she said, taking another quick look at her watch.

"Not quite all . . ."

"I forgot to mention that I fully intend to meet your deadline. Naturally, you'll have final approval of the article . . ."

". . . when it's too late to assign another reporter if it isn't satisfactory," he said, finishing her sentence as she took a breath. "Unfortunately, there's not anything I can do about it now, so you don't have to look at your watch again. I'm well aware of what time it is. Finish your coffee and I'll walk you to the bus."

"It isn't necessary . . ." Her voice trailed off when she saw that he wasn't paying the slightest attention; merely finishing his coffee and pulling out a handful of change to pay the bill. There wasn't any hesitation in his movements. It was irritating because Miranda was still trying to decipher the amount on each coin and hoping to tip the proper amount with the unfamiliar currency. It was plain that her employer was above such "straight-off-the-boat" maneuverings.

He picked up her bags again, heading for the terminal exit before she got off the bar stool. She *did* manage to catch up with him as they went outside into the stifling heat, and tried to sound businesslike as she commented, "I'm sorry that you're uneasy about hiring me for this project."

"Pick another word," he said, not slowing his stride as he marched down the sidewalk toward the parking lot. "Substitute 'madder than hell' for 'uneasy.' Barry knows that I don't go for untried staff on a lead article."

"Aren't you even going to give me a chance?" Miranda's voice rose to a breathless wail as she tried to keep up with him.

"I didn't say that. I merely have to make other arrangements to ensure that I obtain the results I want."

"Then I will get to take the Danube trip, after all?"

"If you weren't, I wouldn't be dragging your bags across this damned parking lot to shove you on the connecting bus. *And* furnishing the cruise tickets," he added before she could remind him.

"We probably should have had something cool to drink instead of coffee."

Too late Miranda realized she sounded like somebody who wrote a household-hints column instead of travel, and the annoyance on Mitch's face showed it. "What in the devil do you mean by that?" he asked, slowing to stare down at her.

"Just that something hot makes you feel the heat more. Unless you follow the theory that it works just the opposite. I'm not really sure."

"Haven't researched it?" He made no attempt to hide his sarcasm.

"Well—no."

"I hope you don't take the same approach in writ-

ing your article for me. Your probationary article,"
he added deliberately. "There'd better be sound background research throughout. Our readers are entitled
to expert, accurate reporting."

By then, he'd started walking again, but it wasn't
such a frantic pace as before. They threaded their
way through the crowded parking lot toward a row
of tour buses against the fence at the far side. Miranda resisted an urge to pull her blouse away from
her damp skin and wondered how on earth he could
stay so uncreased and crisp-looking in the heat. The
only thing that appeared hotter than usual was his
disposition and she had a very good idea that the
temperature didn't have anything to do with it. If it
hadn't been for a free trip down the Danube, it
would have been wonderful to tell such an overbear-
ing creature exactly where he could go.

He must have been aware of her thoughts, because
his expression stayed grim as he finally pulled up by
the open door of a tour bus marked "Passau." "Okay,
Miss Carey, you'll get the chance that Barry seems to
think you deserve." He interrupted his instructions
long enough to indicate her bags to a perspiring
driver who came around the back of the bus just
then. "The lady's one of your passengers. Her name's
Carey," he added when the man pulled a list from his
shirt pocket. "You'd better get aboard," Mitch continued in a lower tone as he gestured her toward the
steps of the bus. "The natives are getting restless."

Miranda gave a startled glance upward and noticed for
the first time the baleful looks which the seated passengers were directing her way. It didn't take an interpreter
to let her know that they didn't appreciate waiting
for a latecomer in the stifling bus. "But I still don't
have my cruise tickets," she reminded him nervously.

"Collect them on board ship. The purser knows all the details."

"And I send my copy direct to Barry?" Miranda asked, lingering by the door despite the presence of the driver, who had noisily closed the baggage section and was checking his watch.

"You'll learn everything you need to know when you get aboard the ship," Mitch said, putting an ungentle hand under her elbow and almost boosting her up the steps.

"But how do I get your okay?" she paused to ask him at the top of the stairs, even though the driver had to squeeze past her to settle in his seat.

"Just relax," Mitch told her, stepping back as the driver started to close the door. "I'll be in touch."

It wasn't much to go on, Miranda thought as she went down the aisle of the crowded bus, ignoring the muttered comments of "At last!" and "Thank God, at least we're out of the parking lot," from two English-speaking passengers. The German and Japanese remarks were fortunately unintelligible. There was an empty seat near the back of the bus and she sank into it, sighing with relief when the air conditioning started to function.

She should have been interested when the tour guide, who introduced herself as a part-time schoolteacher, started rattling off facts and figures about the outskirts of Munich. Unfortunately, the middle-aged woman's remarks were hardly intelligible. After listening to comments like "We'll watch many gravel pits on our way to Passau" and "In time of high water, people rescued themselves in churches on hills," Miranda decided it wasn't worth the effort. She did learn there would be a late lunch stop and she settled back in her seat as close to the air-conditioning vent as possible while contemplating her immediate future.

Apparently Mitch Emerson had decided that he had no choices available. If he'd paid her off in Munich, he would have incurred Barry's editorial wrath and also left himself without a qualified writer for a lead article in an upcoming issue. He'd made it abundantly clear that her employment was limited, but at least it was better than receiving a pink slip and a handshake.

It didn't help that he'd turned out to be the kind of man that she disliked most; too ruggedly handsome for his good—the type who could expect women to be fawning 'round in wholesale quantities. If he'd lived a century before in the rolling countryside of linden trees and onion-domed churches beyond the bus window, he'd have collected a saber scar on his cheek and killed wild boar by the cartful. In those days, he'd have exercised his *droit de seigneur* on every presentable woman within reach, Miranda told herself. Then she grinned as she realized that she was bearing out Mitch Emerson's worst fears about unsubstantiated facts. He needn't worry, she told herself as she settled more comfortably in her seat and leaned against the window. Her article on the Danube cruise would be of such superior quality that he'd be begging her to stay on the staff when he read it.

She drifted off to sleep on that thought and was awakened an hour or so later by the guide's harsh voice announcing that they were arriving in the village of Altoetting for their lunch. A village, the woman went on in strident tones, that was almost as well-known as Lourdes, Fatima, and Loretto as a center of prayer.

Miranda struggled to sit up straighter in the seat, trying to ignore the stiff neck she'd collected while using the window for a pillow. Just then she wished that the tour guide would join the pilgrims who were thronging the sidewalks of the small town as the bus moved slowly alongside. The woman's voice was so rasping that it was difficult to understand even her simple luncheon announcement that they would have an hour and fifteen minutes in the restaurant across the square. If they all ate quickly, she told them, they could visit the small picturesque chapel afterward. As Miranda left the bus, she noted the crush of pilgrims trying to get in the church and decided not to count on it.

The restaurant was a high-ceilinged room half-filled with diners, but the passengers were herded toward empty tables in the corner. Miranda walked to a round table occupied by a young couple and a man with a well-dressed elderly woman. Before pulling out the vacant chair, she asked, "Do you mind if I join you?"

"We'd be delighted, my dear," the elderly woman replied while the nice-looking man beside her bobbed up to seat Miranda with gratifying enthusiasm. "I'm Elsa Miller," the woman continued in a pleasing Southern drawl, "and this is my son Joe."

"Who's only functioning on half-speed right now," replied the man as he sat down again. "I still can't believe we made it in time for the bus."

"At least let people introduce themselves before you tell them our troubles," his mother said with a reproving shake of her head.

"I'm Miranda Carey . . ."

"Is there a Mr. Carey around?" Joe Miller asked, looking as if he really wanted to know.

"Only my father," Miranda said, amused, "and he's in San Diego at the moment."

"Practically our home turf," cut in the crew-cut man across the table, who looked to be in his late thirties. "I'm Farrell Short and this is my wife, Janice," he added, indicating the attractive brunette beside him.

"Farrell's in the Marines," she said, smiling at them. "We were stationed close to San Diego for about a year. Do you still live there, Miss Carey?"

"Miranda, please. It's home base, but I'm hoping for a full-time job in Manhattan." She crossed her fingers as she thought about Mitch and then added, "I'll have to wait and see."

"All parts of the country heard from," Joe Miller said. "Or almost. I'm glad I can understand what you're saying. I couldn't tell whether it was our guide or my ears were plugged after our flight—but damned if I knew what was going on aboard that bus." He broke off as a waiter put some glasses in front of them and then deposited bottles of red and white wine in the center of the table. "This should help things along."

As they watched the serving of the wine, Miranda took the opportunity to study her table companions. Joe Miller's clothes looked expensive and conservative in design; his knit shirt blended perfectly with gray gabardine slacks and yellow cotton cable-knit sweater folded on the back of his chair. He definitely wasn't the kind of man who reached for the nearest thing in the closet, Miranda decided. His tanned skin and neatly groomed fair hair showed they received the same expert attention.

His mother was also beautifully groomed. Her aqua shirt-chemise was apparently impervious to travel mishaps and its lines showed a designer touch. A beautiful diamond solitaire and earrings confirmed that the gray-haired woman was accustomed to the finer things of life. She must have been in her late sixties, but she made no attempt to minimize her age, and wore very little makeup.

"White or red?" Joe asked his mother as the final pourings were completed.

Elsa made a moue of displeasure as she scrutinized the label of the bottle he was holding. "Neither one. Perhaps a little sherry—if that's not too much trouble."

Miranda was amused to see how the waiter who'd only shown a cursory interest in the proceedings until then assured her that sherry would be forth-coming immediately, leaving the rest of the people at the table to sort out their own wine as the main course of veal and noodles arrived.

By then, Miranda noticed that Joe Miller was al-ready pouring his second glass and encountered his mother's amused glance as she shifted hers.

"Poor Joe," the older woman said, "he's feeling the effects of the last eight hours."

"Eight!" Her son shook his head ruefully. "Make. it twenty-eight. At least it seems that long. I thought we'd never get out of New York."

"We missed the plane," Elsa put in when she saw their puzzled looks. "Can you believe it? This son of mine forgot to change his watch when we arrived in Manhattan."

"So there we were waiting in the club at the termi-nal," Joe continued, taking another swallow of wine. "Pretty soon I asked the bartender when our flight would be called. He checked with the receptionist and found it had left twenty minutes earlier."

"So there *we* were," his mother said, "after all the

delays with our Dallas flight and knowing that we had to connect in Munich with this bus or we'd miss the first part of our cruise."

"What happened?" Janice Short asked, wide-eyed, as the silence lengthened.

"Fortunately everybody helped and got us onto another airline with a Munich flight. We came in just an hour after the one we were scheduled on. We even had time to wait in the bus," Joe said with a wicked glance at Miranda.

"I'm sorry," she said, embarrassed by the attention she suddenly was attracting. "I had to meet a man."

"So we noticed," Janice said. "Very nice, too. I was hanging out the window watching—and trying to get some air at the same time."

"However, we'll forgive you now that we've reached a semblance of civilization," Joe told Miranda blandly before giving his attention to his mother. "You should have tried this wine. It isn't half-bad."

"You'll have to do justice to it for both of us," Elsa replied, and turned the subject to a gentle inquisition of the Shorts. It evolved that the couple was on an unexpected vacation since both sets of grandparents at home had volunteered for baby-sitting duties with their grandchildren.

"And we're making the most of it," Farrell Short told them, raking his fingers through his crew cut.

"Farrell's just been promoted to major," his wife announced proudly, "so we're trying to pretend that we can afford a cruise down the Danube. Doesn't it sound great?"

Everyone around the table agreed that it sounded just that. Miranda noted that Joe Miller and his mother had only been to Hungary and Czechoslovakia once, although they apparently had traveled to Austria and

Germany on several other trips. Aside from an abbreviated assignment in England which allowed for some short side trips to France and the Low Countries, it was virgin territory to the Shorts, as well as Miranda.

"And what about you, Miranda?" Farrell wanted to know. "Are you vacationing or visiting family in the 'old country' or what?"

"Honestly, Farrell—this isn't a board of review," Janice protested. "Maybe Miranda doesn't want to answer all your questions."

"I don't mind," Miranda said, pushing back her plate, because it was really too warm to enjoy such a heavy meal. When she professed that hers was just a pleasure trip, their puzzled faces showed their disbelief.

"But don't you mind traveling alone?" Janice probed.

"Now who's getting personal?" her husband chided.

Miranda kept her expression bland. "Just because you start a trip alone doesn't mean that it has to end that way."

"Now that's the kind of answer I like to hear," Joe Miller said, grinning. His mother's eyebrows went up slightly, but she nodded her understanding.

"I should have known," Janice said, brushing back her thick dark hair from her face. "That man who saw you off at the bus—"

"Oh, he's not a friend," Miranda started to say before she thought better of the explanation. There was no way that she wanted to bring Mitch Emerson's position into the conversation just then. "He's not anyone special," she assured Janice. "Just an acquaintance. My cousin asked him to be sure that I got on the bus safely. You know how families fuss— just as if I couldn't find my way out of the airport alone." She leaned back in her chair and added, "I hope the food aboard the ship is as good as this."

After that, the conversation flowed on general lines and Miranda was able to enjoy her dessert—a feather-light lemon mousse.

Once coffee was served and hastily drunk, the Shorts decided to try to get inside the chapel for a look at the altar and perhaps a picture.

Miranda strolled out of the restaurant with the others, but seeing the solid phalanx of pilgrims around the small church, decided it wasn't worth the effort. The Millers felt the same and Elsa announced that she'd prefer to get back on the bus early.

Joe glanced around the crowded square. "If it's parked in the shade, I'll join you. I could certainly use a nap at this point. Before we go, though"—he turned to smile at Miranda—"I wonder if you'd share a table with us on the cruise."

"That sounds very nice," Miranda said slowly, surprised by his offer, but unable to think of a reason to refuse. The Millers were pleasant and it would be nice to see friendly faces in the dining salon three times a day.

Joe's smile widened at her acceptance. "Great! I'll arrange it with the chief steward as soon as we get on board. See you later."

Miranda watched him shepherd his mother care-fully past the people on the crowded sidewalks on the square and smiled. It was reassuring that such old-fashioned courtesy still abounded. Not every man exhibited the dictatorial tendencies of Mitch Emer-son, she thought as she remembered his sendoff in Munich. At least Joe Miller's invitation had helped restore her ego, which had been dented in that other encounter. Having Elsa at the table on the cruise would ensure a friendly holiday relationship without any emotional overtones. Joe hadn't mentioned a wife, but his manner showed that he knew how to handle all ages of femininity very well.

As Miranda strolled back toward the bus by way of an attractive garden just beyond the main square, she found herself wondering if she should mention her writing assignment to the Millers and then decided against it. If Mitch Emerson didn't approve of the final draft, she'd look an almighty idiot with a rejected story. Of course, there was always the chance he'd change his mind.

She uttered an unladylike snort at that possibility and earned a disapproving look from a couple admiring a Stations of the Cross statue next to the sidewalk. Miranda walked on hurriedly and turned in the direction of the parking lot when she came to the garden wall. She'd just have to do the best she could, she told herself, and not hope for miracles.

At that precise moment, bells rang out from the imposing Parish and Collegiate Church. A moment later, she heard more bells tolling from the Church of St. Mary Magdalen nearby.

Miranda stopped short and smiled. It was an uncertain, shy smile and she was unaware of the tremulous beauty it brought to her face.

There was nothing farfetched about hoping for a miracle, after all. Whether by luck or design, for the first time in her life she was in the right place for one!

2

The city of Passau in eastern Bavaria was a pleasant surprise when the bus arrived in the late afternoon.

Translating the guide's garbled English, Miranda learned that Passau was the meeting place for three rivers: the Inn; the Ilz, which she'd never heard of; and the Danube, which she certainly had. Apparently beyond the cobbled streets and stone facades of patrician homes, there was the School of Theology and Philosophy plus the Goethe Institute and University of Passau. There were also, Miranda noted as she peered through the bus window, some familiar golden arches that didn't have anything to do with Old World culture, but were a welcome sight nonetheless.

They had dropped down in elevation from the rolling forested hills surrounding the city, and as they drove past the towers of St. Stephen's Cathedral, she could see some picturesque castle ruins beyond one of the rivers.

There was a buzz of conversation in the bus as the tour passengers looked out, trying to catch the first glimpse of their cruise ship, which was to be anchored at a pier on the Danube. Another sharp turn of the bus and the guide said triumphantly. "There! You see him."

Then, before anybody could ask who "him" was, the woman went on, "The finest ship on the river where you are to be soon."

Miranda smiled and shook her head. Apparently the woman had taken a crash course in conversational English and skipped anything to do with grammar. She could only hope that the crew aboard that impressive "him" had spent longer on their language homework.

Even if they only spoke Tibetan or Kurdish, life wasn't going to be hard to take on such a gorgeous ship, Miranda decided as the bus driver inched his way along a narrow cobbled street next to the river and finally stopped in front of a chained-off area of the pier.

It would have been hard to find fault with the impressive river-cruising vessel tied up just ahead of them, and the guide wasn't about to give the passengers a chance. She herded them off the bus like a bunch of slightly retarded sheep. "So please make a few steps more," she commanded when they lingered near the baggage bays of the vehicle.

When a nervous soul mentioned that he wanted to see what happened to his suitcase, she brushed the protest aside. "It is taken care of. You come this way to your ship." Leading the travelers along the pier, she informed them that their vessel was the newest on the Danube and its sturdy, squat design was necessary for river cruising. Apparently, the navigation bridge and funnel lowered hydraulically and there were anchors at either end of the ship to cope with Danube currents. The name *Donau* was inscribed in bold letters on the bow and Miranda lingered for a

said wryly. "At the moment, I'm still adrift without a cabin, but the purser is supposed to solve all my problems."

"Well, if you have any left by cocktail time, join me in the bar and we'll solve them together."

"I thought you were taking a nap to cope with jet lag."

He shrugged as he started down the stairs again. "There's no point in sleeping and missing all the excitement when we cast off. I'll keep a place for you."

Miranda almost warned him not to count on her and then decided against it. Joe was right, she thought, as she started toward the lounge. There was no point in hibernating in her stateroom. After all, how many times would she have a chance to be cruising down the Danube?

She gave a cursory glance at the decor of the big lounge when she went through the glass doors amidships. There were windows all around the room, which was attractively decorated in shades of plum and beige, with honeyed fruitwood for the tables. Sandwiched in at the bow was a small stage where two men and woman were playing Strauss in subdued tones that didn't interfere with tea being served at some of the tables or champagne sendoffs at others.

Miranda glanced worriedly over the people and then walked to the bar. "Excuse me," she said when she finally got the attention of a gray-haired bartender. "Have you seen the purser, please?"

"*Ja, ja.*" He jerked his head toward the far side of the big room, indicating an alcove which she hadn't noticed before. "You'll find him there."

Nodding her thanks, she followed his directions. There was a uniformed man in the alcove, but he was talking with someone else and all she could see was the back of their heads as they huddled over a table.

Miranda marched up to them before she lost her nerve and said, "I'm very sorry to interrupt, but I'm Miranda Carey and I think that—" As both men got to their feet, her voice trailed off to a gurgle. "My Lord—it's you! What on earth are you doing here?"

Mitch Emerson looked resigned as he gestured toward a chair. "Sit down, Miranda. I've been expecting you. This is Gerhard Schmidt, a friend of mine."

The purser, a nice-looking fair-haired man in his thirties, seemed amused at her stupefied expression and gestured her to a chair. "Will you join us in some champagne, Miss Carey?"

Miranda dazedly shook her head to clear it and decided that alcohol wouldn't help. "No, thank you. I didn't mean to interrupt. All I need is my ticket and stateroom key."

"There's no problem," Mitch told her, reaching into his jacket pocket to put them on the table. "You might as well relax and have a drink. This is a good place to see everything, Gerhard tells me."

"Best view on the river," the purser confirmed proudly. "But unfortunately, I don't have an excuse for sitting here and enjoying it. I'd better go below and make sure our paperwork is up-to-date. The Austrian authorities can be firm if we're out of line. I'll see you later, Miss Carey. Nice to have you aboard, Mitch," he said, getting to his feet and giving them a smile.

Miranda barely let him get beyond earshot before she gave her employer a look that could have put a layer of frost on the big window in front of them. "I knew that you didn't like my assignment to this story, but I thought that you'd at least give me a chance. Or maybe you had second thoughts after putting me on the bus."

His relaxed expression disappeared abruptly as he looked her up and down. "I didn't have second thoughts. I feel precisely the same way I did when I first heard about your arrival. I didn't mention joining you on board then because I wasn't sure if there was additional space available for the cruise."

Her forehead wrinkled at his declaration. "Let me get this straight. You mean you're going to write the story instead of me?"

"Not unless it's necessary." he admitted tersely. "Let's just say I'm keeping a watching brief on you."

"Then I'm still supposed to take the cruise?"

"Good God! Do you want it spelled out in words of one syllable?" Mitch sounded as if he couldn't believe that anybody could be so thick-headed. "You take the cruise as planned and you'll be on your own covering the story until I see the final result."

"But if you're on board too . . ."

He cut into her sentence ruthlessly. "I told you. It's a backup precaution. I have some spare time and I might as well cruise the Danube as spend it in England as I'd originally planned. The weather's terrible there right now and I could use some of this sunshine."

If she hadn't been so annoyed with the man, Miranda would have noticed that there was more than a touch of weariness to his voice and in his face. Instead, her glance dropped to the two small squares of cardboard lying on the table along with the cabin key. "Those say table fifteen."

Mitch's grim expression didn't chance. "So?"

"But that's where I'm sitting with the Millers."

"Who in the devil are the Millers?" he asked, obviously making an effort to hold on to his temper at her newest objection.

"Joe's a public-relations man I met at lunch—something to do with petroleum. His mother's traveling with him." When Mitch's features didn't alter at her pronouncement, she gestured impatiently toward the seating designations again. "The dining-room steward must have made a mistake and double-booked the table."

"Not unless two and two make five." As her eyes widened in disbelief, he added, "I thought we'd share a table since you and I seem to have trouble conducting an ordinary conversation. Gerhard fixed this seating arrangement for us—I suppose they put the Millers there when they mentioned your name. If it's all right with you, it's all right with me."

Miranda wanted to shout that it *wasn't* all right with her. The last thing she wanted at that particular moment was to cruise the Danube with him at her elbow, giving her an acute case of indigestion at every mealtime. Life was too short for such irritations even with a free cruise thrown in. Her lips parted to set him straight on it, but as her glance met his laconic one, her mouth closed again.

"Exactly," Mitch said in a firm tone which indicated that he'd read her thoughts far too accurately. He put one of the table-assignment cards on top of her stateroom key and added a brochure of the ship before handing them over. "I suggest you check out the cabin before we sail."

Miranda picked them up, but kept her glance locked on his. "Are we sharing anything else?" she asked, too annoyed to be diplomatic.

His eyebrows went up. "Exactly what did you have in mind?"

"A stateroom," she said boldly, determined that she'd only go so far to get a job on his staff and that sharing living quarters exceeded her limit. "Four walls with a door that locks."

"That key"—he pointed to the one she was clutching against her breast—"fits the door on a single stateroom. You can lock it or not as you choose. Personally, I make it a point never to mix my business and social life, so if you have any ideas along that line, you can forget it."

It took a moment for his comment to sink in, but when it did, a dull red suffused her cheekbones and she had trouble getting her words out. "Why, you . . . you . . . egotistical . . . imperious—" she began thickly.

"Spare me the histrionics," he cut in, standing up beside her. "Some editorial staffs are run differently, so I won't hold your offer against you."

"Will you listen to me?" she flared, interrupting *him* before he could finish. "I was about to say that I wouldn't consider anything but separate staterooms."

"Of course."

His bland tone made her cheeks turn even redder. "I *mean* it," she said through clenched teeth. "I didn't want *you* to get the wrong idea."

He nodded and made a production out of looking at his watch. "Well, now that we have it all settled, I'm going down and have a nap in *my* stateroom. You don't mind if we're on the same deck, do you?"

There was no attempt to hide his sarcasm and Miranda's chin went up. "Not at all—you should be quite safe. I think I'll stay here until we've cast off. There's no reason why I can't do some of the background research in the lounge as well as my state-room. Besides, I want to take pictures of Passau."

"You don't have to furnish those," he said, sound-ing bored as he turned to leave. "We have file photo-graphs available and the shipping company will supply anything else."

Miranda watched him stride out of the lounge without a backward glance. Almost as if he couldn't wait to put a decent distance between them, she thought. For a moment she wondered whether or not to go below to inspect her own stateroom, but a long blast on the ship's whistle made her sit down again. Already a crew member was hauling in a bow line, so she might as well watch the departure in comfort. There was iced champagne in the bucket at her el-bow, and even as she inspected it, the bartender materialized beside her with a fluted glass, saying, "Allow me, miss." And then when the glass was filled, he smiled and added, "I'll bring over a plate of canapés right away."

Miranda smiled her thanks and leaned back to relax. This was one thing that Mitch Emerson couldn't spoil for her, she decided, and took a swallow from her brimming glass as increased vibration from the engine showed that the *Donau* was finally under way. She watched with enjoyment as a bow thruster took the ship toward the center of the broad river and the charming old-world houses of Passau slipped toward the stern. The picturesque castle on the hill above the river Ilz came into view again as the ship entered the Danube's downriver currents. Miranda reached automatically for the camera in her purse before she remembered Mitch's last comment and sat back in her chair again. If he didn't want her to work, she'd just have to be a lily of the field. The arrival of the plate of canapés reaffirmed her decision and she gave a sigh of contentment as the ship straightened and increased speed in the river channel.

There was a small blast of welcome from a passing river steamer which scheduled daily trips to Vienna, and the *Donau* gave a ladylike whistled response in return. The red-roofed stone houses of the town thinned to nothing almost immediately and even the roads along the riverbank disappeared, to be replaced by tree-covered slopes on gentle hills.

The charming landscape soothed Miranda's spirit in a way that she wouldn't have believed possible, and for an instant she wished that Mitch had stayed a little longer to enjoy it too. Even his irascible nature couldn't have withstood the peaceful countryside with neat farm dwellings, or the fishermen sitting on the banks of the river who waved as the boat passed. Two swans came into view, looking as if they'd just emerged from a Hobbema painting as they glided along the smooth water near the shore.

While the outdoor landscape was serene, the tempo aboard ship was accelerating by the minute. There was a festive air among the passengers as they came in to congregate in the lounge, and the bartenders were kept busy supplying their wants. Miranda glanced at her watch and decided that the cocktail hour was going to be the most popular function on the cruise but since she didn't want to be a part of it just then, she decided to retreat to her cabin.

She managed to reach the stairway without encountering any familiar faces and returned the pleasant smile of a stewardess as she turned down the long corridor on the deck where the purser's office was located. The key Mitch had given her said one-eighteen and she was pleased to find the cabin was almost amidships. That meant the shipping company was either hoping for a favorable article on the *Donau* or that Mitch Emerson's friendship with the purser bore tangible results.

Miranda unlocked her door and drew a surprised breath at the first glimpse of her cabin. The interior walls were decorated in a warm beige and the two sofas in an L-shape along one wall and under the spacious square porthole were upholstered in a cinnamon shade. The wall-to-wall carpet was a slightly darker shade of brown, which blended nicely with the light wood paneling of the bureau and closet doors.

She stepped carefully around her bags which had been put alongside one of the sofa beds and left her purse on the combination dressing-table/bureau before turning to inspect the compact but nicely appointed bath. There were thick rust-colored towels on the racks with a matching mat for the small shower cubicle. "Better and better," she murmured to herself, and wasted another minute sniffing the soap and bath gel on the shelf over the basin.

Back in the main cabin she read the instructions for the closed-circuit color television and switched on the radio located at the end of one of the sofa beds. The only thing she could possibly find to criticize was the strength of the bulb in the table lamp. But that was easy—she'd simply give up reading in bed and enjoy the rest of the amenities instead.

She set about unpacking and stowing her belongings without wasting any more time. Fortunately, most of her clothes weren't too badly creased and she decided on a deep red jacquard-patterned dress with long sleeves for her first dinner aboard.

There was time for a shower, she decided, and

carefully locked the cabin door before peeling off her clothes. Afterward she padded back out to the cabin swathed in an outsize towel and sat down on the sofa under the porthole to relax for five minutes before getting dressed for dinner. It was a good time to check out her notes on Durnstein, the ship's only port of call before Budapest. From what Mitch had said, he expected her to have all the facts at her fingertips and probably wouldn't be averse to checking her knowledge over the soup course.

The history of the Austrian town with its tiny population of only 533 inhabitants was unexpectedly interesting. After reading about the ruined castle on the hill where Richard the Lion-Hearted was held prisoner by Duke Leopold in 1192, she started making notes for her article in earnest and she could hardly believe the time on the face of her travel clock when she heard the chimes for dinner in the corridor outside.

She set a new record for dressing, but she was still the last one at their table when she arrived at the dining room a little later.

"I was afraid you'd been thrown in the brig or whatever they call it aboard ship," Joe Miller said, getting to his feet and smiling at her as she pulled up breathlessly beside the table. "Mitch was going to give you five more minutes and then go pound on your door."

Miranda directed a cool look toward her employer, who'd gotten to his feet and was holding her chair for her. "You needn't have worried," she assured him, sitting down. Then her voice warmed as she smiled at Elsa across the table. "I'm really sorry to be late. I hope that you aren't starving."

"Nonsense, my dear." Elsa looked much more refreshed after her rest and as well-groomed as ever in a tailored silk shirtwaist of emerald green. She gestured with a half-full sherry glass. "Joe and I just brought our drinks along."

"Which reminds me," Joe said, picking up his wineglass and raising it to Miranda, "you missed the cocktail hour and some tremendous scenery. Mitch told us you were working, though."

"Then you've all met," Miranda murmured in polite inquiry.

There was a noncommittal mutter from Mitch at her side, who kept his attention on the big menu, but Joe beamed across the table.

"Lord, yes. The purser did the honors in the lounge. I don't know why you had to be so havey-cavey about your writing assignment, Miranda. Mother and I certainly can keep quiet about it." He pursed his mouth thoughtfully. "I suppose you didn't want Farrell and Janice to noise it around. A couple who had lunch with us," he said when Mitch's head came up inquiringly.

"It's just a job, after all," Miranda murmured, and felt a moment's annoyance when her employer's stern mouth quirked in amusement. He knew very well why she'd kept quiet, she thought bitterly. Her hold on the assignment was just about as slippery as the shrimp appetizer a waiter was trying to serve at a neighboring table. Fortunately, his actions served to divert their attention to the more important matter of dinner, and conversation shifted to whether shrimp in dill sauce would be preferable to apple slices with Roquefort dressing.

Aside from the chef's tendency to serve cherries atop everything—whether veal or lentil soup—the dinner was delicious. Certainly it seemed to do miraculous things for Mitch's disposition; he showed a talent for pleasant dinner-table conversation that left Miranda almost speechless. He probed her opinions on the political situation in the bordering Danube countries and then just as skillfully extracted the feelings of the Millers on the subject.

Elsa volunteered the information that she'd originally come from Germany, but had lived in Oklahoma so long that she'd almost forgotten about her roots.

"I wouldn't have dreamed it from your accent," Miranda said, marveling.

"Sounds like a real native, doesn't she?" Joe said proudly.

"Well, you certainly do," Miranda said, smiling.

"That's not surprising," Elsa said, putting down her fork to take a sip of the German white wine which Joe had decided they all should be drinking with their dinner. "He's lived in Oklahoma all his life except for a year or two in New York."

"The big city beckoned and my wife decided that was where we should live. It didn't last long," Joe said, brushing a crumb from his navy-blue blazer.

"I didn't know you were married," Miranda said in some surprise.

"I'm not. It didn't last long either," Joe replied with a shrug that signaled an end to that topic.

"Joe came home to do a very good job in public relations," Elsa told them. "It's turned out well for us."

"I see." Miranda wondered if there were any small Millers still in the picture, but couldn't think of a diplomatic way to ask and then forgot about the subject as Elsa continued, saying, "It was a big help for his father to have Joe take over in the family business. Especially when he was so ill. He died just recently."

"I'm sorry to hear that . . ."

Elsa gave a decisive little nod, acknowledging Miranda's sympathy. "Fortunately, we have some very competent help to run things while we're away. Otherwise, I wouldn't have left home."

"Nonsense, Mother. You needed a vacation. There would have been another patient to look after if you'd kept on without a break. You know that's what the doctor said."

Elsa turned to beam at him and then directed her attention across the table again, including Miranda and Mitch in her smile. "Joe's always been so considerate. I can't tell you how I depend on him."

The dinner took longer than usual since the final course was a dessert buffet which had passengers lining up to choose between strudels and ice-cream delicacies. Miranda had a little of each and vowed that she'd be more sensible for the rest of the voyage or she'd roll down the gangplank at the end of the trip.

As they left the dining salon, Mitch announced that he planned on taking several turns around the deck to work off some of the calories. Elsa cut in to say that she was heading back to her stateroom to see if she could sleep off the remnants of jet lag that were still plaguing her.

"I think I see the Shorts heading into the lounge," Joe said, craning his head to be sure. "Miranda, how about joining them?"

"I really have to do some more research," she said weakly, when it became apparent that Mitch wasn't going to help her out. Not that she expected an invitation to join him, but he could at least confirm the fact that she was working.

"Forget it. You don't have to be so conscientious, does she, Mitch?" Joe asked, sweeping her objections aside in masculine fashion.

"Naturally, it's up to Miranda," her employer replied in a couldn't-care-less tone.

"Then I'd love to talk to Farrell and Janice," Miranda said defiantly, taking the offensive.

"I'll say good night," Elsa told them moving toward the stairs.

"All right, Mother," Joe said solicitously. "I'll check in a little later and see you're all right." After making sure that his mother had successfully negotiated the steep stairs, he turned to Miranda and Mitch. "Sometimes she forgets that she's not as young as she thinks. How about joining us in the lounge later on, Mitch?"

"Not this time." Mitch glanced at his watch and then said calmly to Miranda, "I wouldn't make too much of a night of it if I were you. We dock at Durnstein in the forenoon and there's a lecture about the port before we arrive."

Apparently the diplomatic manners he'd exhibited in the dining salon had disappeared and he'd returned to his usual terse ways. "I saw it in the bulletin," Miranda told him coolly, "but I've already read up on Durnstein."

He stared back at her, his features unrevealing. "Good. Then I won't have to worry. 'Night, Joe."

"Seems to be a nice fellow," Joe said heartily as he steered Miranda toward the lounge, which was rapidly filling with passengers who were loath to miss any festivities aboard ship.

Miranda thought privately that her employer more closely resembled Torquemada interviewing prisoners during the Inquisition. Fortunately, she remembered to be discreet and returned Joe's smile, saying,

"*Isn't* he!" with proper enthusiasm. "Do you suppose there's a place to sit?" she asked, changing the subject when they hovered at the entrance of the lounge.

"Farrell and Janice will have saved us some seats," Joe assured her, craning his neck. "Ah! There they are—right next to the dance floor. The combo should be starting any minute now."

"I don't think I should stay too late," Miranda said, trying to keep up with him as he pushed through the tables toward the center of the room.

"Nonsense! This is playtime," Joe said in a masterful manner over his shoulder. "I never believe in letting duty get in the way of having fun."

For a mild-mannered man, he showed an unusual streak of determination. Miranda was even surer of it an hour later when she found herself sipping champagne she didn't want and dancing with him. The dance floor was crowded with ship's officers who tried to pretend that entertaining the passengers was what they really wanted to do in their off-duty time, but their gaiety sounded thin.

Miranda would have pleaded weariness and escaped to her stateroom during an intermission except that she noticed Mitch had been annexed by the ship's hostess after his stroll on deck. The attractive Frieda was staying close by his side and had even gotten him on the dance floor.

He acquitted himself very well for a man whose chauvinistic ideas dated from the Neanderthal days, Miranda decided reluctantly. Fortunately, he stayed on the other side of the lounge when he wasn't on the dance floor and the only time his gaze encountered hers, he'd looked pointedly at his watch.

This gesture had inspired her to promptly accept another glass of champagne and move her chair closer to the ship's engineer who had joined Joe's party. The engineer's English was of the same variety as that of their guide to Passau, and Miranda found it difficult to keep her eyes open during his longer anecdotes.

When the combo finally packed it in for the night several hours later, she was so tired that she could hardly find her way down to her stateroom. The fact that Mitch's tall figure wasn't in view was her only solace at that point.

Even that was small consolation for an aching head. After thrashing around for an hour, she searched for some aspirin so that she could get a little sleep. The realization that she'd have to appear bright-eyed and alert at breakfasttime made her groan aloud as she surveyed her reflection in the bathroom mirror.

So much for the vaunted blue Danube, she thought bitterly as she stomped back to bed. So much for romantic Europe—so much for men in general. And, at the moment, that damned Mitch Emerson in particular.

3

Under normal circumstances, the prospect of a sunny summer day would have made Miranda smile, but the eruption of her alarm clock after a bare three hours' sleep did little to start the morning off right. The buzz of the travel alarm reverberated in her ear like a thirty-two-foot pipe in the organ at Westminster Abbey, and she bounced upright to try and stop the commotion.

The sudden movement made her clutch her head, and she moaned as the bright sunlight streaming through the porthole hit her eyelids with the force of a laser beam. She managed to shut off the alarm and drag the curtains across most of the window before falling back against her pillow to muster strength for the hours ahead.

It had been a mistake to have that champagne, and the aspirin she'd taken in the middle of the night hadn't dented her throbbing headache. At any other time, she would have chalked it up to experience and turned over to try to sleep it off. But even with her eyes closed, Mitch's warning of the night before tolled in her ears like the doomsday bell. There was nothing for it but to get up and explore Durnstein—come hell or high water.

She dragged herself out of bed and went toward

the shower, unable to ignore the realization that she had only herself to blame. If she'd just stopped off in the lounge and then gone sensibly to her stateroom as she'd planned, instead of letting the sight of Mitch and that miserable ship's hostess cause a change of plans, she wouldn't be in trouble.

Miranda turned on the shower at full force, hoping the tepid water would wash away memories as well as clearing her head.

It helped to the extent that later she was able to don some white slacks with a turquoise T-shirt and stopped only once to clutch her head. Slacks would be the perfect thing for a walking tour or exploring deserted castles, she decided, and smothered a groan at the thought.

As the breakfast chimes sounded in the corridor, she applied some lipstick and tried to ignore the fact that it only served to accentuate her pale cheeks.

She couldn't believe her good fortune when she reached the dining room and found the table deserted, with the place settings untouched. A few moments later, the waiter informed her that neither of the Millers would be in for breakfast, having told him the day before that they preferred their morning meal in their staterooms.

"What about Mr. Emerson?" Miranda asked, trying to sound as if she didn't care either way.

"I don't know, Miss Carey. He didn't say anything last night, so I imagine he'll be along."

Miranda nodded, concluding that her only salvation would be a very fast meal, consumed before her employer could appear. "I'll have toast and coffee, thanks," she told the waiter as she returned the menu to him.

"No fruit or juice?"

Miranda's glance lit on a table across the aisle, where four German passengers were wolfing down a platter of cold meats and bread. She shuddered at the slices of blood sausage on their plates and said faintly, "Just a small glass of orange juice to start."

She was finishing her second cup of coffee a few minutes later when Mitch appeared and pulled out a chair across the table. "Good morning," she said, trying to sound cheerful and briskly efficient. "I've finished, so I was just leaving." The last came as she patted her lips with her napkin and pushed back her chair to stand up.

"Don't let me detain you," he said dryly.

She shot him a quick glance, but by then he'd focused his attention on the menu, apparently intent on the breakfast choices. "I'd keep you company," she said, lingering in her chair, "but there's still some reading I want to finish before we tie up in Durnstein."

"I'm not surprised," Mitch said, putting down the menu and fixing her with an unwavering scrutiny.

Miranda's eyes narrowed as his comment registered. Even in her hurry to depart, she was conscious that he looked as if he'd had his full quota of sleep. His short-sleeved burgundy knit shirt was without a wrinkle and the glimpse of his chino trousers showed a knife-edge crease. Probably that brunette hostess had arranged for him to get special service at the laundry, Miranda thought bitterly. Then, aware that the silence was getting embarrassing, she asked, "What do you mean by that crack?"

"Merely that you didn't have time for hitting the books last night." His gaze surveyed her slowly, not missing an inch on the way. "It appears that you didn't sleep much once you reached your stateroom. I wonder if you're up to this Durnstein visit? There's considerable walking involved—and a steep hillside if you plan to visit the castle."

"You mean the one where Richard the Lion-Hearted was incarcerated in the dungeon and Blondel, his minstrel, located him so he could be freed after a ransom payment?"

"So the story goes. It's a nice bit of trivia."

Aware that Mitch wasn't impressed by her attempt to show off, Miranda switched to a safer approach. "Well, I certainly intend to check it out and the rest of the town, too."

"Then I suggest you skip the lecture. Go down to your cabin and rest until we get there. At the moment, you don't look as if you'd make it to the end of the gangway."

He turned his attention back to the dish of grapefruit segments that had just been put in front of him. The momentary diversion allowed Miranda to make her escape, her cheeks flaming at his sendoff.

The fact that he was right made it all the more difficult to accept, and she slammed the door of her stateroom behind her, wincing at the noise. If Mitch Emerson thought he was going to accompany her at Durnstein and make her entire day miserable, he had another think coming, she told herself as she walked over and sat down on the sofa bed under the porthole.

In the meantime, it wouldn't hurt to follow orders and rest for a while. Before she stretched out on the cushions, she made sure to set the alarm again—allowing plenty of time to be the first one off the ship at Durnstein. After a productive and highly professional viewing of the village, she'd come back aboard in triumph and show Mitch the fruits of her labors.

It was a most satisfactory plan and Miranda fell asleep thinking about it without any trouble at all.

When she awoke the next time, her headache had subsided and she was able to look through the port-hole at the picturesque Wachau section of the Dan-ube with real pleasure. The hills were steeper than the Passau area and more heavily forested—allowing only the spiny rock ridges coming down to the wa-ter's edge to show gray and brown earth tones among the shades of green. Occasionally, an energetic farmer would have terraced the steep hillsides so that they resembled the vineyards of the Rhine, but it was the exception rather than the rule. The bright sunshine reflected from the white onion-topped churches of the Austrian villages which looked so neat and clean that they resembled travel posters extolling the gran-deurs of the country.

Miranda set about in a methodical way, collecting her tiny camera, her big over-the-shoulder handbag, plus a notebook with a pen and pencil. At the last minute, she stuffed in a ship's brochure on "Things to See" and then let herself out of the stateroom, locking the door behind her.

The lower decks of the ship were almost deserted and when she learned from a passing stewardess that they were docking in Durnstein within ten minutes, it was easy to see why. Apparently most of the passen-gers were up on the open sundeck, where they could view both sides of the river.

Miranda knew that was the last place she wanted to be—since both the Millers and Mitch were surely in attendance. She went back down the stateroom corridor, where she could see two stewardesses talk-ing. It didn't take much persuasion or a very big tip to be allowed off on the crew gangway as soon as the ship was tied to the pier. Miranda merely knotted a kerchief over her hair and kept her head down, staying in the middle of the off-duty stewardesses as they surged ashore. Since Mitch wouldn't be expecting her to be with them, she didn't have to worry and, as added insurance, the public-address speakers on the ship were announcing that the passengers' town tour wouldn't be leaving for another twenty minutes.

She parted company from the crew at the first refreshment stand they encountered on the riverside walk, leaving the others to wait for their friends. Keeping a steady pace, she made for the outline of buildings which appeared to be the center of the village. Unfortunately, they were all located at the top of a steep cliff bordering the river, which meant that she'd have to find a stairway to reach Durnstein proper. For a moment, she regretted her hasty departure from the ship, since the tour bus was supposed to deposit the passengers right on the main street, avoiding the steep climb.

Then she told herself severely that some inconvenience had to be expected to achieve the results she wanted. It was a pity, though, that the castle she needed to explore was considerably further up the hill and past the main part of the town.

She'd only gone a few hundred feet along the tree-shaded walk when she saw a sign with an arrow pointing toward the cliff. Moving behind a refreshment stand, she discovered a stone stairway leading upward.

It was dark and the steps were crudely fashioned, but she stuck close to the wall and tried to guard against a misstep in the gloomy tunnellike aperture. After climbing two long flights, there was a landing where she could view a hotel terrace which overlooked the river. It was well filled with Durnstein citizens, who were enjoying in the pleasant shade of umbrella tables for their early midday repast.

The steep climb had made Miranda's headache return with a vengeance and she looked longingly at the terrace, thinking how pleasant it would be to enjoy a cup of tea in the flower-bordered restaurant, and then shook her head as she remembered the work she still had to do.

Three more steep flights of stairs finally brought her out on a cobblestone side street of the town, and she sat down on a bench with a sigh of relief. To the left, she could see the outlines of the former Collegiate Church, which she identified by the guidebook she'd hastily shoved in her purse. If she went that way, she'd also be able to tour the remains of the Klarissin Convent.

She got to her feet and started up the street, ignoring souvenir counters and barely glancing at the picturesque town houses constructed from the sixteenth to the eighteenth century. Fortunately, the sunlight made it easy to snap pictures to accompany her note-taking, and she finally lingered to admire a vine-grower's cottage with its low doors and the dated plaque which extolled the town's rich history.

When she'd covered most of Durnstein's town center, she cast another look up the steep hillside to her right, where the ruin of the castle stood out starkly in the sunlight. The only path up to it didn't look easy and Miranda decided there should be enough time in her schedule for a cup of tea on that shaded terrace. After that, she'd tackle the rigorous climb.

Richard the Lion-Hearted would certainly understand, she told herself as she turned back down the cobbled street. After all, he probably hadn't been in a hurry to reach it himself.

Her only pitfall would be a chance encounter with Mitch, but he probably wouldn't be wasting his valuable time under a gaily colored umbrella. Unless, of course, the ship's hostess had convinced him that the terrace was the best place to enjoy the pleasures of Durnstein.

That wasn't a possibility to dwell on and she strode resolutely back down the narrow street, retracing her earlier steps. There were undoubtedly other entrances to the hotel, but rather than waste time searching for them, she'd use the stairway landing she'd encountered earlier.

It wasn't hard to find the end of the gloomy tunnel, but the dense shade after the bright sunlight had her almost blinded as she started down the irregular stone steps. She immediately slowed her pace, clutching the side wall for a guide. If the Durnstein Chamber of Commerce had a suggestion box, she'd certainly put in a request for a railing, she thought irritably as she started down the second flight. By then she could make out partial sunlight outlining the landing leading to the terrace.

She let out a breath of relief as she finally reached the landing and then turned into the other stone tunnel with the terrace at the end of it.

She was so intent on reaching her destination that a sudden noise behind her caught her completely unaware. Even as she whirled in shocked surprise, two hands grasped her around the waist and ruthlessly shoved her back toward the stairway she'd just left. She was propelled to the shadowed, deserted landing and then suddenly pushed ruthlessly down the stone steps.

Miranda shrieked in terror and threw out her hands as she hurtled forward. For an instant, her fingers clutched at an old iron ring which had weathered the centuries and she clung to it desperately as her body slammed into the wall. The ring slipped from her nerveless fingers from the force of the collision and she landed on the steps in an untidy heap, whimpering with pain.

She could feel blood trickling down her arm as she huddled there—fighting the giddiness trying to overtake her and finally losing, as even the glimmer of light in the old tunnel abruptly turned to complete darkness.

4

"What the bloody hell!"

The masculine voice was familiar, Miranda thought, but it couldn't compete with the pain that engulfed her and it was easier to keep her eyes closed—hoping whoever it was would go away and let her try to cope on her own.

Then she felt firm hands on her shoulder, tugging her into an upright position against the wall, and her eyelids went up reluctantly. "Leave me alone," she protested, trying to draw away from the intruder. "Just leave me . . . Oh, Lord! It would be you." The last came as she recognized Mitch's grim features inches from her own.

"God in heaven!" His words were a measured monotone, barely audible even on the deserted stair. The grip on her shoulders tightened, relaxing only when he felt her wince under the pressure. "I'm sorry." He drew a deep, uneven breath. "Look, you can't stay in this moldy place."

"I know." Miranda tried to brush her hair from her face and then stopped abruptly as she felt grit on her cheek. "Damn! I must have a handkerchief some-place," she said, starting to feel around her on the step for her purse. "I just need to clean up a little."

Mitch let her know what he thought of that in two pithy words that made her stare at his stern face. When she felt his hands start over her in a comprehensive inch-by-inch search, her eyes went wide.

"What do you think you're doing?" she flared angrily, trying to refasten her bra and pull her T-shirt back down to her waist.

His fingers moved inexorably around to her back. "Does it hurt anywhere when you breathe?" he asked, completely ignoring her protests, pushing her hands aside when she attempted to stop him.

Miranda took a deep breath before answering, not wanting to let him know that his exploring touch wasn't helping her recover from shock. "I . . . I don't think so."

"Either it does or it doesn't," he informed her in a rough tone. "Make up your mind."

"It doesn't," she snapped back.

"Then it should be all right for you to get up. Wait a minute," he added, transferring his examination to her legs. For all of his efficiency, his touch was gentle and Miranda noticed that his expression was concerned as he saw blood oozing from her skinned knees.

"It looks worse than it is," she said, surprised to find herself reassuring him, but determined to be truthful. "You don't have to worry, I won't put these slacks on my expense account," she added, trying to lighten the atmosphere.

"That's made my day. Hang on to me and we'll get out of this place." He looked around the gloomy tunnel as he pulled her upright. "The hotel here is closest—"

"I'm not going out on that terrace looking like this," Miranda protested, trying to escape his grip.

"Cut that out," he ordered, his hold tightening. "For God's sake—be reasonable. You can't walk back to the ship and I don't think there's a hospital in the middle of town even if I dragged you up to the top of these stairs. You don't have to worry about anybody seeing you—there's a back entrance to the hotel for employees. We'll duck in through there. That way, you can do some makeshift repairs and I can call a doctor."

He had been urging her up the stairs to the landing as he spoke, but his last words caused her to pull back again, even though the effort made her wince. "I don't need a doctor and I'm certainly not going to be stuck here in Durnstein and miss sailing with the ship," she said.

"Don't be a stubborn fool! If you think I'm going to let you go on with the cruise after passing out—"

"I did *not* pass out," she informed him, her chin at a defiant angle.

"And I suppose you didn't collapse on the stairs," he retorted, not bothering to hide his sarcasm.

"That's the first thing you've gotten right," she said. "But I didn't fall—I was pushed."

Mitch was so startled that he forgot to hang on to her for an instant and she staggered before he clutched her to his side again. "Would you repeat that?" he asked, lingering in the middle of the landing to stare intently down at her.

"I was pushed." Miranda's anger had disappeared by then and there was no doubting her sincerity. "I'd just turned in here to have a cup of tea. Somebody came up behind me and the next thing I knew I was taking a nose dive down the steps."

"You didn't see whoever it was?"

She shook her head regretfully, but held his gaze.

"It happened too fast. It must have been deliberate, though. Nobody's stolen the hotel silver or made off with the cash box in the last hour or so, have they?"

"Not that I've heard of," he said, urging her toward the hotel again. "I'll ask around when we get inside. The manager's a friend of mine."

A sudden thought struck Miranda as she moved gingerly beside him. "You didn't happen to notice anybody near the stairs, did you? Before you came across me?"

"No—unfortunately. Nobody special, that is. Half the ship's passengers were on the terrace at one time or another. The tour stopped here for coffee." He sent her a quick sideways glance. "As you'd have discovered if you'd done what you were supposed to do."

Miranda ignored that, sticking stubbornly to her line of thought. "So 'most anybody could have followed me onto the landing. They'd have been perfectly safe behind all this shrubbery." She gestured toward the high box hedge along one side of the path.

"I'm afraid so." Mitch turned her toward a door in the building instead of going on to the terrace. "This is the entrance I was talking about."

"But it says '*Verboten*.' "

"That just means it's for employees," he said, opening the door and shoving her ahead of him. "Besides, when did you start following rules?"

"You're not being fair," she snapped, and then lowered her voice as two hotel chefs in towering white hats turned to stare at them. "I was just trying to do my job."

Mitch marched her ahead without commenting and

Miranda relaxed only when they passed another door and found themselves out in the carpeted foyer. "There's a ladies' room over there," Mitch told her, gesturing. "Sit down on this chair and I'll get somebody to help you into it."

"That isn't necessary," Miranda assured him, shaking off his grip and standing erect. She discovered that her headache was pounding away and her skinned knees stung horribly, but otherwise things weren't bad. "Honestly, Mitch—I can manage to wash off the grime."

"Well, go in and get started," he said reluctantly. "I'll phone for a cab and check with the hotel clerk to see if there's a homicidal maniac running loose in town."

His words made Miranda halt abruptly with the rest-room door half-open. "You won't be far away, will you?" Then, regretting her sudden weakness, she tried to pass it off lightly. "In case my maniac's still on the prowl."

"Don't worry—I'll keep an eye on you from now on."

That admonition would normally have brought her back fighting, but just then his words were remarkably comforting and she nodded before going in the immaculate cloakroom to try to become presentable.

Barely five minutes passed before a gray-haired lady in a starched hotel uniform appeared, carrying a plastic box with a big red cross on the side of it. "Mr. Emerson thought you would need assistance," she said in barely accented English. "If you will just sit down in that chair," she went on, frowning as she surveyed Miranda's appearance. "You will allow me, please."

Miranda decided that the woman must have been a retired children's nurse, because she certainly knew how to take care of bloody knees and scraped elbows. The antiseptic she applied stung like crazy, but it would have been a strong germ which would have dared to linger in the circumstances.

"I am sorry there is nothing I can do for your clothes," the woman said ruefully, surveying Miranda's torn and stained slacks.

"You've been wonderful. Don't give it another thought—I'll put them in the round file as soon as I get back on the ship."

"The round file?" The woman's English apparently didn't cover American slang.

"I'll just throw them away," Miranda told her, managing to find some paper currency in her purse that she could slip in the woman's pocket as they strolled to the door. "Thank you again."

Mitch was standing in the hotel's well-furnished foyer, a troubled look on his face, which cleared as he saw her approaching. "I was wondering if I dared come knocking on the door," he said, taking her elbow and steering her toward the entrance. "There's a cab waiting for us."

Miranda was glad to note that he avoided the steps which led down to a tiled lobby filled with leather furniture and some rare-looking Oriental rugs. The one couple they encountered in the foyer looked hastily away after catching sight of Miranda's stained clothes.

"So much for our reputations," Mitch said lightly, seeing a flush spread over her cheeks. "They'll probably regale their friends with an account of drunk-and-disorderly tourists."

"In that case, it's a good thing we're leaving town." Miranda pulled up at the door of the taxi which was waiting in the hotel drive. "There's no reason for you to cut short your stay ashore. I'll be perfectly fine once I change clothes. Maybe I can even get back to visit the castle."

"Don't be a damned fool." Mitch gave her a gentle shove into the worn back seat of the taxi and followed on her heels. "I have the address of a doctor—"

"No way," she said, cutting into his words so emphatically that he stared at her, momentarily surprised into silence. "I mean it," she went on, and leaned forward to address the taxi driver. "The ship, please. The *Donau*," and gestured toward the river in case he didn't understand. When he nodded and stepped on the accelerator, she sat back in her corner of the cab and risked a glance at Mitch, who was bristling with disapproval. "Look—I know you mean well," she began apologetically, but still determined that she wasn't going to let herself be sidetracked for a few aches and pains. When he did nothing to break the thick silence, she tried again. "I wouldn't be so stubborn if there was anything really wrong. And I promise I'll stay aboard for the rest of the day—" She broke off as a disquieting fact surfaced. "—except that I really need to visit that castle for my article."

Mitch exploded then as he told her in a very few words exactly what he thought about that.

Miranda wilted under his attack, aware that he couldn't be pushed any further. "Well, I suppose I could use a reference book, except that I did want to see where Blondel was suppose to have serenaded him."

He ignored her last tentative plea. "If that's all that's bothering you, the magazine has a comprehensive set of file pictures which should be more than adequate. Provided the assignment goes as planned."

"You don't give an inch, do you? I've never known anybody who was so prejudiced."

"That's one hell of a remark. You're lucky to even be here. If I'd used any sense, I'd have paid you off and booked your return flight at the airport in Munich."

Miranda thought it best to change the subject before he followed the same impulse in Budapest. "I do appreciate getting a chance, but you can't really blame me for getting pushed down some stairs." She glanced toward him as another thought occurred. "Was there an idiot loose in town today?"

"Not that anybody at the hotel has heard of. They promised to get in touch with the police, though—just in case." Mitch looked out as the taxi slowed and pulled to a stop in a parking area above the pier where the ship was tied up. "Seems as if everybody's still ashore," he said, noting the empty decks and deserted gangway.

"Thank heaven for small favors," Miranda muttered as she opened the cab door on her side and tried not to wince as she stepped out. Mitch paid off the driver, who slammed the doors and got back in the car again after shaking hands enthusiastically with both of them. "You don't have to come with me," Miranda said as Mitch steered her toward the gangway.

"I wish you'd stop telling me what I don't have to do," he stated with a wry grimace. "And stop looking so annoyed. Otherwise that fellow"—he jerked his head toward the uniformed sailor who was on duty beyond the end of the gangway—"will think I'm responsible for the way you look."

"That's not funny . . ."

"You're right—it isn't." He marched Miranda through the heavy glass door to the air-conditioned interior. "Let's have your cabin key."

By then, Miranda was too tired to put up any

more objections and fumbled in her purse, managing
to find the key by the time they'd gone down the
deserted corridor and stopped at her stateroom door.

Mitch ushered her inside and watched her sink
onto the nearest divan before saying, "You look as if
you could use a cup of tea. I'll see if I can rout
somebody out. In the meantime, stay put."

Miranda made a rude face at his back as he disappeared out into the corridor again, and then groaned
as she caught sight of her bedraggled figure in the
dressing-table mirror. A colorless complexion and
lank hair weren't helped in the least by her dirty and
bloody outfit. God knows, she needed more than a
cup of tea, she thought unhappily as she got to her
feet and started peeling off her clothes.

She left her slacks and shirt on the carpet and
discarded her nylon underthings when she reached
the bathroom. Even the tepid spray of the shower
stung on her grazed skin. She felt so light-headed at
one point that she had to hang on to the soap dish for
support, but at least she was clean when she turned
off the water five minutes later.

She was dabbing carefully at her bruises with a
towel when she heard the corridor door open and she
threw a quick look at the bathroom door to make sure
she'd slid the bolt.

"Miranda?"

There was no mistaking that voice of authority.
She let out an unconscious breath of relief. "I'm in
here."

"You're supposed to be out *here*."

She quickly slid back the bolt and opened the
bathroom door just a crack. "I'll be there in two
shakes."

"You'd better be, or the tea'll get cold."

Miranda suddenly discovered that she hadn't brought any clean clothes in with her and frowned as she thought about it. She certainly didn't want to ask him to go through her lingerie drawer and closet to supply the missing links.

"Are you coming?"

Mitch didn't hide his impatience and Miranda looked frantically around the steamy bathroom—finally focusing on a thigh-length white terry robe hanging from a hook on the door. It was furnished by the steamship company as an added amenity for passengers, and she pulled it on gratefully.

An instant later, with it belted tightly, she stepped out into the stateroom.

Mitch was staring out the big porthole, ostensibly engrossed by the green hills of the Wachau Valley. He turned to face her when she closed the bathroom door, appraising her deliberately from her bare toes to her damp, tousled hair. It seemed to Miranda that he lingered longest at the lapels of her robe, and she felt her cheeks grow warm under his amused masculine regard. When she noted that he'd picked up her slacks and shirt from where she'd discarded them on the floor to put them in a neatly folded pile atop the dresser, her cheeks grew redder still. Probably he'd concluded that she threw her clothes around all the time, she thought angrily, and made sure there was a safe overlap of her robe—especially at the lapels.

A moment later when he said, "I'd suggest that you lie down on that bed before you fall flat on the floor," she deduced that seduction certainly wasn't on his agenda. As she started to follow his orders and caught another glimpse of her disheveled self in the mirror, she almost laughed aloud. It was a wonder he'd even bothered to bring the tea in person rather than send a stewardess. By the time she'd propped herself up on the closest divan, he'd unearthed a pillow and an extra blanket from the other and brought them over. Miranda found herself nuzzling his chest momentarily as he leaned down to pull her forward so that he could push the pillow behind her back. Then, without a wasted motion, he turned and tucked the blanket around her legs. "That should do it for the moment," he said, surveying her as he straightened.

Miranda suspected that he'd have the same satisfied expression if he'd wrapped a package for mailing without leaving any loose ends. She surveyed her cocoon of blanket irritably. "I feel like Cleopatra wrapped for delivery."

"Except that she was rolled in a carpet . . ."

"And Mark Anthony is among the missing," Miranda told him with smug satisfaction. Then she remembered her reflection and her shoulders drooped. "That was a silly remark. Forget it."

"You'll feel better when you get some of this inside you," Mitch said, going over to pour a cup of tea. "I hope you like it straight because I forgot to bring any milk or sugar."

"It doesn't matter," she said, reaching for the cup and taking a sip. "Umm, that tastes good." She looked up to see him lounging on one corner of the dressing table, apparently content to watch and make sure that she was following orders. "Aren't you having any?"

"I'd just finished some coffee up at the hotel before I found you."

"That seems a long time ago." She concentrated on the pale liquid in her cup. "You don't have to hang around," she managed finally, still keeping her glance down. "I promise I won't leave the ship if that makes you feel better."

"It does," he drawled, "but I'm not taking any chances."

A sharp knock on her stateroom door came before Miranda could ask what he meant, and she stared when he moved quickly to open it. "Dr. Koenig?" he asked, seeing a stout gray-haired man dressed in a dark suit and carrying a leather bag.

"Quite right. I gather you are not my patient," the doctor said, hovering on the threshold. His English was fluent and bore traces of a British teacher.

"Miss Carey suffered a bad fall on one of the stairways in town," Mitch said, gesturing toward Miranda. "She claims she's fine, but I'd feel better. . ."

". . . knowing for sure," the doctor concluded, coming in to stare down at her with a kindly expression. "It's safer that way. I'm sorry that Durnstein didn't treat you better, Miss Carey." He put his bag on the dressing table and opened it purposefully. "This shouldn't take long."

"I'll be outside," Mitch said, ignoring Miranda's baleful glance as he reached for the doorknob. "Probably at the purser's office," he told the doctor as he lingered in the corridor. "I'd appreciate it if you'd check with me there."

He was gone before Miranda could say a word, and after that, she didn't have time to dwell on her employer's high-handedness.

Dr. Koenig was one of the old school and took his medical calling seriously. Miranda was poked, prodded, and subjected to a barrage of questions before the doctor grudgingly admitted that an overnight rest would see her back to normal by the time the ship arrived at Budapest the following morning. "And you are fortunate," he said as he left a tube of salve to apply when she removed the bandage from her knees the following day.

"I know," she said, almost giddy with relief that she'd passed the medical barrier. "As pretty as Durnstein is, I didn't want to miss the rest of the cruise."

"That, too," he agreed. "But I meant that the consequences from a fall on that stone stairway could have been much more severe. There are any number of former patients in town who'll confirm what I say. I hope you'll be more careful for the rest of your trip."

Evidently he hadn't heard the whole story, Miranda thought, and decided it was just as well. At that moment, all she wanted was to be on board when the *Donau* set sail for Hungary and Budapest.

"I think it best if you take this pill now," the doctor added, dropping it into her palm. "No, don't get up. Allow me," he said, pouring ice water from the carafe atop the dressing table.

"What's it for?" Miranda asked as she took the glass he held out, but hesitated before swallowing the pill.

"To ensure a good rest—nothing more." He waited until she'd swallowed it and then put the glass back beside the carafe. "It's quite fast-acting, so don't get far from that bed in five minutes or so. *Guten Tag, Fräulein* Carey," he added briskly as he closed his bag and carried it to the cabin door. "I'll let Mr. Emerson know about your condition so you won't have to worry about that. Just rest and let nature work her miracles."

Miranda frowned in dismay as he went out into the hall, closing the door behind him. She pushed a strand of hair back from her hot face and tried to think what she should do in the four and a half minutes she had left. Damn the man! Damn all doctors! Why hadn't he warned her before she'd swallowed the pill?

She tugged at the bedspread, trying at least to get the bed properly turned down if she was going to spend hours in a horizontal position. Even then, it was an effort and she felt a lassitude slowly creeping over her.

Suddenly it seemed like too much work to hunt for her sleep shirt and slippers. There was nothing wrong with sleeping in the robe she had on. It was a shame that it was so bulky, though . . .

She was still considering that when Mitch came back into the room and surveyed her frowningly. "From what the doctor said, I thought you'd be flat out."

Miranda focused on him with some difficulty. "If thass so . . ." she began, aware that she was having trouble enunciating. "If that's so," she repeated more carefully, "what in hell are you doing in here?"

"Ever gracious." He stared at her in some amusement. "I shouldn't give you a bad time, though. The doctor said you were still experiencing delayed shock. I know I am."

"I'm glad to know that it won't last for the rest of the trip," Miranda said slowly, thinking how little it would take for her to start sobbing against the first available shoulder. "I still hate to waste . . ." Her voice trailed off as she tried to remember what she was talking about. She closed her eyes momentarily to think.

"Hey! Don't fall asleep now."

Mitch's voice barely penetrated her consciousness

and it was an effort raising her eyelids to stare at him in owllike fashion. "Who's fallin' 'sleep?" she demanded querulously.

"Who do you think? You'd better get out of that robe right now or . . . Damn!" His last exclamation came as he saw that her eyelids were down again, clearly to stay. And she wasn't comfortable, he thought, that was obvious at a glance—propped up against the pillow with that toweling robe rumpled under her and the blanket trailing onto the floor.

Mitch stared at her relaxed figure a moment longer, his glance lingering on the almost classical beauty of her features. Even the violet shadows under her eyes highlighted her pale ivory skin tones as she lay so quietly. She shifted slightly on her pillow at that moment and the reddened graze on one cheekbone came into view. Mitch's mouth compressed in an ominous line and he muttered something that would have made Miranda's complexion change color if she'd overheard. He continued to stare as she moved restlessly again, trying to find a comfortable position. That prompted Mitch to go over and open the door to the corridor. After a searching glance up and down the deserted hallway, he came back in, locking the door behind him. Five minutes later he retraced his footsteps and this time went out in the corridor, checking to make sure that Miranda's stateroom door was again locked securely as he pulled it tight behind him.

5

Sunshine seeping through the curtains of her stateroom window awoke Miranda the next morning. She stared around the empty room as if she'd never seen it before and then the events of the previous day came flooding back and she sat up abruptly. That brought a twinge of pain and she touched her face experimentally, only to discover that the graze on her cheek still was painful if she didn't treat it gently.

A burst of laughter came through her door from the hallway, along with the sound of running footsteps. Miranda swung her legs out of bed to walk across the stateroom and see what was happening in the world outside. There were houses and buildings everywhere on the gently rolling hills seen through her porthole, and Miranda drew in a delighted breath as she realized they must be approaching Hungary's famed capital. To think she might have slept through all the excitement!

She hurried toward the bathroom, shedding her satin sleep shirt as she went. Then suddenly her fingers became motionless in the process of hooking it on the back of the bathroom door. The toweling robe she'd worn yesterday hung there neatly and Miranda frowned as she stared at it. If memory served her right, she'd been wearing that robe when the doctor left. Strange that she couldn't remember changing clothes when she could recall what an insurmountable task it seemed at the time. And it was stranger still to realize that she'd managed to not only don her sleep shirt, but methodically put away the robe as well.

Miranda stared at the robe for a moment longer and then slowly shook her head. There was no use trying to fool herself that any such thing had happened. Someone must have helped her. Her color rose as her mind flipped instantly to the only person on the scene to work the miracle. But even he wouldn't have the nerve to act as lady's maid under the circumstances.

Her subconscious let out a raucous cheer at that realization. Mitch Emerson had nerve to spare, and a little thing like removing a woman's clothes wouldn't give him a moment's pause. In fact, she would have bet her next month's salary that her employer was well versed in all details of the female form. Not only that, most women of his acquaintance probably wouldn't have shown the slightest reluctance at removing their clothes in his presence.

Miranda slammed the bathroom door closed. She'd be damned if she'd ask the man what had happened, although she was tempted to see if her stewardess had been recruited for the job.

As she turned on the shower, Miranda decided she might be making too much of the matter. Her view of the Danube's banks near Durnstein had shown that Europeans didn't go into nudist colonies to follow their chosen way of life; they simply lounged on the shore of the river and often stood up to wave enthusiastically when the ship passed by. The little matter of a sleep shirt paled by comparison.

She toweled herself dry a few minutes later, taking care to pat the grazes that still throbbed, and didn't waste any time slipping into her clothes. Fortunately, she'd packed a blue-and-green cotton belted with a colorful sash. The dress was both cool and comfortable when teamed with a pair of woven leather flats. Carefully applied makeup helped subdue the scratches on her cheek, and her full skirt hid the worst of the abrasions on her knees.

She dabbed on some cologne, made a last check in the mirror, and then grabbed her key before hurrying out in the corridor.

There were just a few souls entering the dining salon, showing that most of the passengers felt as she did; nothing was going to interfere with their arrival in Hungary's first city. Miranda went out on deck and hurried to the forward stair, wincing just slightly when her bruised knees protested at such treatment.

Even that was forgotten as she reached the open observation deck and was able to glimpse the magnitude of Budapest spread out on either side of the Danube. The captain of the *Donau* was evidently enjoying the tableau as well, because the ship was making its way slowly and there was so little river traffic that it couldn't have been a deciding factor.

At that moment, she heard footsteps from behind and turned to discover Mitch surveying her, a frown on his face. "I had a feeling I'd find you up here," he said. "At least it was worth a try before I had the stewardess check out your stateroom."

"How did you know I wasn't there?" The words were out before she stopped to think, and she grimaced at his involuntary grin. "I know. The telephone."

"And the door. I knocked on it until I was afraid your neighbors would complain."

"Sorry," she began automatically and then caught herself. "No, I'm not. I'm not unhappy about anything this morning. Isn't this marvelous?" She gestured at the impressive scene around them. "I don't know why, but I didn't think Budapest would be this big."

"Over two million people. That's quite a bunch." He leaned against the rail and pointed to the left side of the river. "The big building over there contains the Houses of Parliament. It's on the Pest side. The land in the middle of the Danube just off our stern is Margaret Island—sort of a refuge for city dwellers. That's where their big sports complex is located, together with the opera and the ballet. Nowadays it's connected to the 'mainland' by a bridge which was put up in place of a nineteenth-century span. The Germans were responsible for its destruction in 1944. Unfortunately, their demolition charges exploded too early and caught quite a few innocent citizens in the mess."

Miranda stared thoughtfully back at the bridge in question. "The history books seem still open over here, while at home they're regarded as closed chapters." She turned to survey the Parliament building with its neo-Gothic arches and great dome silhouetted against the sky. "That looks bigger than Buckingham Palace—the architect must have been paid by the square foot."

Mitch's crooked grin appeared for an instant. "It's possible. At one time it was supposed to be the largest building in the world. The dome is the same height as the basilica—to put church and state on an equal footing." He shot a quick glance at his watch. "If you want to have any breakfast, we'd better go below. You can look out the window down there just as well. And don't say you're not hungry," he added before she could protest. "If you're going to wander around Budapest, you'll need food inside you. I take it that you do plan to stay upright for a while."

The last came as he surveyed her carefully. Miranda was sure that he didn't miss the shadows under her eyes, which the Durnstein doctor's prescription hadn't banished. "I feel fine," she said, lifting her chin defiantly.

"If you practiced that line, you might make it more convincing. Never mind—I know this is one argument that I'm destined to lose."

Her own lips quirked. "You're right there. About the only way that you could convince me to miss Budapest would be to put a padlock on my stateroom door."

"Like yesterday, you mean," he said, gesturing her ahead of him toward the stairway to the lower deck.

"You can't be serious . . ."

"I didn't mean it literally." He gave her a gentle nudge when she stopped to stare at him. "I did ask your stewardess to keep an eye on things—just as insurance."

She stopped again—this time at the head of the stairs. "In case somebody aboard the ship gave me a shove yesterday? Good Lord! You can't be serious."

"Well, I didn't lose any sleep over it," he said, sorry that the subject had surfaced. "It just made sense to cover all the possibilities. But now, in the light of day"—he looked toward the sky, where the sun had momentarily hidden behind a cloud—"it seems as if I overreacted."

Miranda's grasp on the stair railing relaxed with his words. "I'm sure you did. Probably I just got in the way of some idiot in a hurry. I'll have to make sure that I give the stewardess a good tip for her extra duties." She glanced over her shoulder at him as she started down the stairs. "What did you tell her to enlist her services?"

"Just that you'd had too much to drink up in the terrace beer garden," he replied after the briefest pause.

She pulled to an abrupt stop. "You didn't!"

"Look," he said with exaggerated patience. "You ask a stupid question—you get a stupid answer. Get going, will you? I'd like to have breakfast before we dock." He moved around her on the stairs and kept a firm grasp on her wrist until they reached the dining room. "What do you know," he said conversationally then in a low voice. "Looks as if our table partners have decided to join us in honor of the occasion."

Elsa Miller, wearing a black-and-white dress with dolman sleeves, was immaculate as always. She beamed at them as they approached. "Good morning—good morning. Joe, dear—help Miranda with her chair. How are you feeling now, child? I heard what a dreadful experience you had yesterday."

Miranda tried to sort out her comments for one proper answer and decided it was no use. Joe, nattily attired in a black linen sport shirt and gray slacks, came around the table to drop a hasty kiss on her nose. "You look wonderful in that dress, honey," he said, and made a ceremony of pulling out her chair. "The only thing that made me get up at the crack of dawn," he went on, "was hope of seeing you."

"You mean that bacon and eggs didn't have anything to do with it?" Miranda teased him as she sat down. She indicated the platter in front of his place. "That looks awfully good."

"I think so myself," Mitch agreed, sitting down

and waving away the menu. "Shall we make it two more orders, Miranda?"

"I usually just have toast and coffee . . ."

"That's not a good way to start the day," Elsa cut in, her brisk voice at odds with her years. "Especially when you need to get your strength back after being in bed."

"Mother and I would have called on you last night, but your chaperon warned us away," Joe said, waving his fork toward Mitch. "You don't mind if we go on with our breakfast, do you?"

"Oh, please do. Cold eggs are awful," Miranda said hastily.

"Then we'll try for hot ones," Mitch said as the waiter hovered. "Scrambled?" he asked Miranda.

It was too much trouble to protest, and besides, the faint aroma of bacon from Joe's plate made her realize that she was incredibly hungry. "Scrambled will be fine."

Elsa waited until they'd been served with orange juice and coffee before she said, "I thought you'd get up today—especially since you haven't been to Budapest before."

"Miranda was so busy taking in all the sights on the observation deck that I had trouble dragging her away," Mitch said.

"I wasn't the only one." She gestured toward the stragglers coming into the dining room. "They barely made it, too."

"The weather isn't bad—a little warm for getting around, but it could be worse," Joe commented, reaching for a piece of toast.

"You sound as if it's old hat to you," Miranda said, after taking a last swallow of her juice. "Am I the only newcomer here?"

"Well, it's been a while since I visited," Elsa said, pulling her coffee cup closer. "Joe was here when he toured with friends—how long has it been?"

"Three or four years," he replied. "Nothing appears to have changed."

"From what I could see of the buildings, nothing's changed in the last three or four hundred years," Miranda said. "It's like going back in time."

"If you mean the dirt of the ages hasn't been removed, I agree," Joe said, his expression cynical. "Or didn't you notice the gray cast over most of the city?"

"I just noticed that it looked old—and interesting," Miranda told him. "To be honest, I can't wait to go ashore."

"Make sure that you have your visa," Joe advised. "It's not quite as strict here as some of the other Eastern countries, but—"

"—it pays to follow the rules," Mitch confirmed. He gave Miranda a sideways glance. "Did you collect all the necessary bits and pieces from the purser's office?"

"I will." She sat back so that a generous serving of bacon and eggs could be put in front of her. "Provided I ever finish breakfast."

"Well, if you'll excuse me—" Elsa said, pushing back her chair. "There are a few things I want to do before I go ashore."

"I'll come with you, Mother," Joe told her as he got to his feet. "Although there's no use hurrying. We're too late in docking to get any bargains at the market."

"What else is there to do?" Miranda asked. "I haven't had time to read all the brochures."

"Well, there's shopping on Vaci Utca and plenty of places for coffee. If you're in the mood for a

Roman Bath, there's a good one across the river," Joe said with an amused expression. "I'll be happy to serve as your guide."

Miranda felt Mitch stiffen at her side and she said hurriedly, "Perhaps another time—I'm really here to work." She risked a hesitant glance at her employer's stern profile. "Although I'd certainly like to buy some of their famous Herend china."

"I imagine you can spare five minutes or so for that," Mitch replied, keeping his attention on his breakfast.

Joe lingered by Miranda's side. "Well, at least plan on going to the Lido with me after dinner. We'll have to do something to paint the town red." When she started to laugh, he added, "That was a terrible pun—sorry, strictly unintentional."

"Joe, I'm going on ahead," Elsa said, obviously impatient to be on her way. She spared a moment longer to give Miranda and Mitch a smiling nod. "We'll probably meet ashore. Tourists are apt to congregate in the same places."

"I'll be right with you," Joe said as she started for the door. "What about tonight, Miranda?"

"I'm not sure of my plans," Miranda said hesitantly, wondering why Mitch didn't interrupt and help her out. She waited another moment and then flashed a bright smile up at Joe's hovering figure. "Thanks, I'd love to. I wonder if it's anything like the Lido in Paris?"

"Not if you're expecting naked women," Mitch spoke up unexpectedly. "This one's a different ball game."

Even Joe stared at him. "I never thought of that. You mean no decadent Western weaknesses are allowed?"

"Let's just say that the Soviet-bloc officials have different ideas of nightclub fare from the French," Mitch said, choosing marmalade over a jar of honey. "Unless things have changed radically in the last year."

"Well, we might as well go see," Joe said, after thinking it over. "Don't you agree, Miranda?"

She was aware of Mitch's sardonic gaze on her as she replied, "It sounds like fun—I'll look forward to it."

"Fine." Joe gave her an approving pat on the shoulder. "I'll see you at dinner and we'll take care of the details afterward."

Mitch watched him go out the door before pushing his plate back, as if he'd suddenly tired of marmalade on cold toast. He surveyed Miranda then and said, "I don't suppose that it would do any good to suggest that you give up your busy social schedule and get a decent night's sleep. You won't be missing a thing except some third-rate vaudeville acts that wouldn't rate more than a tryout in Vegas."

Miranda's chin went up defiantly. "It seems to me that I've been sleeping most of the time since I came aboard," she informed him, trying to sound light and uncaring, but not succeeding very well. "I plan to do some extracurricular sightseeing during the day."

"Such as?"

"Well, women readers would certainly be interested in the public markets or handicrafts in the small specialty shops. Places you don't see on organized tours."

"Next you'll tell me that the men will be interested in Budapest nightlife." When she merely stared back at him, Mitch folded his napkin and tossed it on the table. "All right, I can't argue with the human-interest

angle. Readers always appreciate a fresh approach.
I'll be ready to leave shortly."

Miranda drew in her breath sharply. "You mean,
you're coming with me?"

"For part of the day, at least." He got to his feet
and pushed his chair in with a decisive gesture. "I'll
meet you by the gangway in half an hour if that's all
right with you."

"Well, naturally, but—"

He cut into her protest. "Don't forget to bring
your visa. You probably won't need it ashore, but it's
the safest way."

She nodded, although her lips were tight with
annoyance as she watched him stride out of the dining room. "Damn! Damn! Damn!" she muttered to a
piece of bacon on her plate. It wasn't that she had
anything special planned for a day ashore, but Mitch
certainly wasn't the type of man who'd be happy
trailing at her heels as she window-shopped and wan-
dered the streets trying to get the flavor of the city.
Then her eyes narrowed thoughtfully. If she really
dragged her feet while looking for bargains in the
Intertourist shops, Mitch might very well decide that
he couldn't take standing around all that time. With
any luck, she would be able to shake off his disapproving figure in an hour or so and spend the rest of
the day on her own.

When she reached the end of the gangway exactly
a half-hour later, Miranda had her plan of attack in
hand—as well as a straw hat with a floppy brim to
shield her from the sun. As soon as she'd ventured
out on deck, she found that the humidity rivaled
Manhattan's and thanked her stars that she'd put on a
comfortable cotton dress. Even Mitch gave an approving nod as he left Frieda's side to meet her.

Miranda was delighted to note that the hostess's flattering ship's uniform couldn't disguise her flushed complexion.

"Either she's in a rotten temper or the humidity's bothering her," Miranda commented as Mitch joined her by the rail.

He glanced idly over his shoulder. "Must be the humidity," he said, turning back. "She was giving me a rundown of all the best bargain places. I told her she should have been talking to you."

Only, the hostess wouldn't have been quite so interested in that, Miranda thought with amusement, watching the brunette head back inside to air-conditioned quarters. "Maybe I can check with her later," she said noncommittally.

"Right." He was giving her what she'd mentally tabulated as his "employer-to-employee" look. "I'm glad you thought to bring a hat. This sun's hotter than you'd think, even with a slight cloud cover."

Miranda noticed that he didn't seem concerned by the sun baking his own head, since his only concession to the temperature was a short-sleeved rust sport shirt and khaki cotton slacks. His tanned skin at the open-throat collar showed that he was no stranger to hot weather. Probably even the humidity wouldn't bother him, she thought, resisting the temptation to tie her hair back from her hot cheeks with the scarf she'd tucked in her purse.

"Do you need to carry all that?" Mitch was asking as he glanced at her bulging shoulder purse, which could have doubled as an overnight case.

"Unfortunately, yes. There's a camera in here, among other things," she said, trying to adjust the strap so that it wouldn't wear a groove in her shoulder. "Also passport, traveler's checks, notebook, sun-

glasses . . ." Her voice trailed off as she saw him pull
his own sunglasses from his shirt pocket and put
them on. Her glance went swiftly downward, taking
in the trim fit of his slacks at the hips. Obviously he
wasn't carrying all of his worldly goods with him. "I
thought you said we had to have our visas and pass-
ports," she said accusingly.

Without a word, he reached in the open throat of
his shirt and pulled out a flat nylon packet suspended
from his neck by a thin silver chain. "Not the handi-
est place," he said calmly, putting it away again, "but
it serves the purpose. I'll carry your camera for you—
that should help lighten your load."

"I'll be all right . . ." she assured him hastily, not
wanting to take advantage in any way.

He opened his mouth to reply and then evidently
thought better of it. "Whatever you say," he agreed
smoothly, and ushered her ahead of him across the
gangway.

A blast of heat came up and hit them as they
crossed the broad cement expanse of Belgradrakpart
where the *Donau* was tied up. It was apparently the
designated spot for river cruisers, because there was
an older Bulgarian cruiser beyond their bow and
even as they watched, a sleek modern craft with a
Russian flag on the funnel was maneuvering to dock
by their stern.

Mitch turned Miranda toward the flight of stone
steps leading up to a busy street which edged the
Danube. "We'll go to the left for the better shops."

"But what about the museums and state buildings?" she asked, surprised. "Don't forget, I'm on
assignment."

"You haven't let me forget it for more than five
minutes at a time. This way, you'll be doing me a

favor, because I've seen all the things you're supposed to, but I could use help with some shopping."

"Are you serious?" Miranda asked, scarcely able to
believe her luck. She'd always heard that men like
Mitch didn't go shopping; they were the kind who
patronized expensive specialty stores with personal-
ized services where centerfold salesgirls fetched and
carried for them.

"I have a couple of maiden aunts who are determined armchair travelers," he informed her, shatter-
ing her high-flown illusions. "They send a list with
me every time I leave home. Originally, I'd planned
to check out the shopping at Szentendre when we
visit it tomorrow."

"You mean that artists' colony on the river?"

He nodded. "But maybe this china that you mentioned would be a better choice—if I can get it home
without any breakage. I'm not keen on carrying dishes
around."

"You can always have them sent. Although I usually end up carrying things in the middle of my
suitcase wrapped in my only decent pair of pajamas."

His lips quirked. "That wouldn't work for me."

"Not enough room in your suitcase?"

"No pajamas." Something flickered in his glance as
he looked at her, and then was gone again. "But we
can cross that bridge when we come to it."

She nodded solemnly, trying to ignore her suddenly flushed face. "Or you can plan ahead—we
could check for pajamas first off. And if Hungarians
don't wear them . . ."

He sent her an amused glance. "What then?"

"Well, a flannel nightshirt would work just as well."

"My God, don't even mention flannel in this

weather," he said, urging her on up the steps. "We'd
be tagged crazy Americans for sure."

"You have a point," she admitted. "Hunting for
flannel anything at this time of year might be difficult."

"Like trying to find wall-to-wall carpet in a Da-
mascus bazaar." He looked both ways as they reached
the top of the steps and directed her across some
streetcar tracks to reach a sidewalk. "There's a traffic
light down at the corner. We'd better cross there.
Pedestrians *don't* have the right of way in Budapest,
so don't go trying for miracles."

Miranda nodded, noting that while the cars weren't
exactly bumper-to-bumper, the traffic was erratic
enough to make Mitch's comment valid.

"I think the best spot for shopping will be at one of
the big hotels here on the Embankment," he was
saying. "So, if you don't mind walking—"

"Of course not," she supplied when he looked at
her inquiringly. "What's a little humidity?"

"We'll take it slow." His eyes narrowed thoughtfully as a car in the curb lane hesitated for a traffic
light and then surged ahead. "The Millers must have
made other arrangements." Seeing Miranda's puzzled
expression, he went on. "They were in the blue car.
Did they say anything to you about hiring transportation for today?"

"No." She had to hurry to keep up with his strides.
"Why? Is it important?"

"Not really. Maybe I'm just being nosy. Frieda
was telling me that she had quite a conversation with
Mrs. Miller last night."

"I didn't think that our dear hostess wasted any
time talking to female passengers."

"Meowrr."

She flushed at his very creditable imitation of an

alley cat, and said, "Sorry. That wasn't very charitable of me, was it?"

He shrugged. "Actually, I don't think you're far off the mark. But that wasn't what interested me about Frieda's comment. Apparently she overheard Elsa speaking very good German to Joe."

"I'm surprised." Miranda pursed her lips as she thought about it. "But I don't know what it proves. After all, she was born there, so maybe she'd tried to keep up her fluency and to teach Joe over the years. Or they could have taken a crash course in conversational German before this trip, like a lot of people. The major and his wife apparently did that too."

"I know." Mitch grinned down at her. "I heard her practicing on the bartender at that hotel in Durnstein."

"I didn't know they were on the terrace too."

"Oh, yes. Practically the entire passenger list of the *Donau*. I found that out when I was asking around yesterday—while you were enjoying your beauty sleep." He frowned suddenly. "Probably it would have been a good idea if we'd hired a car today too. There's no sense in your overdoing things."

Miranda stopped in mid-stride and gazed up at him, wide-eyed. "Hey, wait a minute! I'm your unwanted employee—remember? Don't start treating me like a director of the company or I'll have a relapse right here on the concrete."

"If you don't pipe down," he said, taking a firm grip on her elbow to urge her forward on the crowded sidewalk, "you can certainly count on it."

"Well, I must say that I appreciate the change, so don't go back to being all cold and stony," she said, swerving to avoid a street cleaner who was sweeping the sidewalk with an ancient broom. "At least, not for a while."

"Maybe we can make it a mutual attempt at role reversal."

Miranda clutched at the olive branch before he could retrieve it. "I'd like that." For an instant she wished that they were walking hand in hand like the couple ahead of them, and then brushed the idea aside. She should be thankful for even small miracles.

"You don't have to give up talking entirely—I just meant for you to curb your more impulsive measures."

There was amusement underlying Mitch's drawled comment and she grinned in response. "I'm still pinching myself to make sure I'm here." She gestured toward the old impressive buildings across the river and then indicated the modern hotels ahead of them on the Embankment. "You know, I didn't realize there'd be such a difference in architecture."

"Over there is Buda," he explained, "where the pricey neighborhoods are. This side is Pest—for shopping and commerce. If you live along here, though, you tell people you live in Budapest—you don't shorten it."

"Sort of 'wrong side of the river' instead of 'wrong side of the tracks'?"

"Precisely," he said, sounding amused again. "But I don't think it'll make any difference when it comes to buying china. What's this Herend stuff you mentioned?"

"Hungary's pride and joy," she told him, happy that she could find a subject where she knew more than he did. "You can buy it in most of the big cities worldwide now, but the prices here are supposed to be the best."

"What's so great about it?"

She shrugged. "It's hand-painted for one thing.

And I guess I just like the patterns. Maybe your aunts wouldn't care for it, though."

"I'm inclined to follow your judgment," he said, steering her to a low concrete building attached to a modernistic hotel which occupied the better part of the block ahead of them. "We might as well start at this Intertourist shop." He waited until they descended a short flight of steps with display cases on either side featuring stereo equipment and other small electrical luxury items before saying, "Don't expect to find the natives shopping here. These shops are strictly for the visitors—they only accept hard currency, and most of the prices will be in U.S. dollars."

"It does take away some of the romance."

He snorted at that and gestured around them as they arrived at a well-stocked shop where salesgirls held small calculators in their hands as they served European and American shoppers.

"I gather the help speaks English," Miranda muttered in an undertone.

"Plus Zulu, Hindustani, or even ancient Greek," Mitch replied wryly. "They're not about to miss a sale. The government wants all the hard Western currency it can get these days."

But not enough to sell separate pieces of Herend china, Miranda found out a few minutes later. If she'd required a service for twelve, there would have been no trouble. "I only wanted a cup and saucer— something like that," she told Mitch disconsolately when they trailed out of the shop empty-handed a few minutes later. "And your aunts wouldn't want a whole set of china."

"You're right about that, and I'm sure as hell not going to drag a tea set home as overweight luggage." He pulled up as they reached the sidewalk again.

"Maybe the shop at the next hotel has a different set of rules. Herend is attractive stuff, though—I can see why you like it."

She started walking beside him. "It's fun looking through the shops, although it would be nice to see some 'home-grown' things."

"You'll have a better chance at that when we go to Szentendre tomorrow." He steered her past a bench at the edge of the sidewalk, where an older Hungarian couple was enjoying the river traffic. "The town's part tourist-oriented and part valid. Actually, any chance to view the Margit Kovacs collection is worth the trip." Seeing Miranda's puzzled expression, he went on to explain. "She was one of the world's leaders in ceramic art when she died a few years ago, and her reputation is still growing. You'll like the exhibit."

"I don't know why you don't write the article for your magazine yourself—I feel like a slow learner when I listen to you."

"Now, what brought that on?" he asked, sounding amused again.

"I'd never even heard of . . . of . . . what's her name?"

"Margit Kovacs?"

She nodded, her expression wry. "And I thought I'd done pretty good research on this part of the world."

"So you learn something all the time. There's no reason to go into a decline about it. I'd never heard of Herend china." His lips twitched as he glanced down at her. "It pays to pool your ignorance."

"That's hardly an apt comparison. Now what's the matter?" The last came when he pulled up short on the sidewalk with a muttered curse.

"I haven't time to explain." He was drawing her into his arms as he spoke. "Just play along, will you?"

The next thing she knew, his lips were nuzzling her ear, blazing a sensuous trail along the side of her neck. Sheer shock kept her in his embrace at the beginning, but that was soon replaced by another feeling entirely, and her arms went around his neck so she could pull his head even closer.

She was oblivious of their surroundings by the time his lips moved tantalizingly up to her face in a series of butterfly kisses, and her eyes closed in blissful anticipation of his mouth covering hers. She waited breathlessly, and then, even in her bemused state, realized that the pause had dragged out too long.

Her eyelids went up slowly and widened when she discovered that Mitch wasn't staring in equally bemused fashion down at her. Instead, his narrowed gaze was directed over her shoulder.

She drew back, still confused but aware that he wasn't suffering from the same breathless state. Her suspicions were confirmed when he said, "That did the trick," in a satisfied tone and absently loosened his clasp. He met her glance for the first time then and a tide of color washed up over his cheekbones. "I didn't mean to spring that on you, but Frieda is hard to turn off," he muttered.

"You mean our hostess from the ship?" Incredulity made Miranda's voice rise.

"That's right. I don't know whether she was hoping to join forces with us or what, but at least now she's taken the hint."

Anger erupted in Miranda like a geyser—a hot unreasoning anger that she didn't stop to question.

"And you made a public spectacle out of me just to brush off your girlfriend! I can't believe it!"

Her raised voice brought curious glances from passersby and Mitch's face reverted to its usual stern lines. "Pipe down, for God's sake! There's no need to tell the world about it."

She bestowed a scathing glance which scattered the onlookers before she turned back to him. Not attempting to hide her annoyance, she snapped, "I object to being used. Next time you're bothered by one of your conquests, you might have the decency to—"

"To what?" he interrupted as she paused for breath. "Lay her out in lavender instead? I was trying to spare her feelings with an example rather than words. Term it a survival technique."

"As if you needed help on that score! My God, you could teach survival techniques to lion tamers."

"Thanks very much . . ."

"You must have come equipped with it at birth," she went on, ignoring him. "I feel sorry for any woman who gets within range."

"I gather that's all you have to say on the subject," he replied, his tone implying that it had damned well better be.

Her shoulders went back and she took a deep breath, trying to match his dispassionate attitude. "I'd prefer going on my own for the rest of the day."

"My thought exactly," he concurred without hesitation. "Would you like me to put you in a taxi before I leave?"

"Not at all," she said airily. "I plan to check out a couple more of the hotel shops, but I don't want to detain you."

"You're sure that you feel up to it?" he asked, like someone who'd just remembered his manners.

Miranda decided his concern was too little and too late. Besides, she wouldn't have admitted a weakness then if her next breath depended on it. "I'm just fine," she told him, taking a firmer grip on her shoulder bag. " And for what it's worth—Frieda's heading for that cab stand over there. If you've changed your mind, you can share a ride with her—provided she's still interested." Miranda started off down the sidewalk, adding carelessly over her shoulder, "I'd simply tell you to get lost."

The words had hardly left her lips when she heard sudden footsteps behind her and a strong arm whirled her around.

Mitch caught her chin in a firm grasp. "If I'd had any sense," he snarled, "that's what I would have told you at that espresso bar in Germany. But don't press your luck, lady—I can still dispense with your very debatable services here and now—provided I don't toss you overboard first. God knows, it's what you deserve." His mouth came down to cover hers then in a painful, grinding kiss that was meant as punishment all the way.

It didn't last long. She was pushed away just as forcefully and left swaying in surprise while he strode back down the sidewalk. Her fingers came up to touch her bruised lips and she gave a furtive glance around, surprised that none of the passersby had noticed anything out of the way. Then, drawing an uneven breath, she managed to continue toward the hotel.

It wasn't surprising that Mitch had picked up the gauntlet she'd verbally tossed at him. Subconsciously, she'd intended him to all along, since it seemed important to her wounded ego. She hadn't expected anything like that last kiss, though—that savage challenge of arrogance and subjugation.

Miranda's niggling suspicions told her that perhaps she was lucky, after all. If they hadn't been in a public place with a goodly portion of Hungarians looking on, her employer would probably have turned her over his knee and administered his idea of punishment that way.

As things were, there wasn't victory or defeat on either side, she told herself—and only wished she believed it.

6

After such a beginning, naturally things didn't improve during the day. Miranda tried to drum up enthusiasm for the gift shops in the next two hotels she visited along the Embankment, but didn't succeed.

She encountered the same story each time—as far as the Herend china went, if she didn't want an entire set, she was out of luck. She gazed at the attractive pieces in the display case, winced at the prices, and moved on.

She stared without interest at the stereo equipment on sale, and a collection of pipes next to a small shelf displaying toiletries. Evidently Budapest hotels catered to travelers who'd forgotten their toothpaste or after-shave. At a price, she discovered, and drifted out to the lobby.

That closely resembled another lobby of the same hotel chain in London and was a clone to one on Central Park South. Even the language wasn't all that different. Bits of English, French, and German wafted around her and the hotel clerks exhibited an impersonal facade that was an international trait.

Miranda walked out to the cab rank at the rear of the building and found a taxi driver who had a smattering of English. With a few verbs and considerable arm-waving, he agreed to take her across the Danube

for a look at the Buda side of the city. They headed
for one of the bridges, allowing Miranda to peer
down where the *Donau* was berthed. At least she
remembered the Hungarian name of the docking place,
in case she couldn't find an English-speaking driver
when it was time to come back.

They wound up the hillside on the other side of
the river. After a few minutes, Miranda decided that
the surroundings were definitely a mixed bag, rang-
ing from staid neo-Gothic buildings to an unusual
statue of a man nude except for his hat.

A little further on, she asked the driver to let her
out at the Fishermen's Bastion—a flamboyant collection of arches and turrets built in the early twentieth
century.

The walkways of the imposing site were teeming
with visitors intent on exploring the nooks and cran-
nies while availing themselves of the wonderful view
of the Danube in all its glory far below. A tour guide
was explaining in loud accented English how the
Bastion happened to be named for the fishermen in
the first place. Miranda learned that the site used to
be that of a medieval fish market. Sometime during
the eighteenth century, the fishermen had decided to
defend the fortification and thereby had earned the
gratitude of the townspeople.

"Now, you will come with me and learn about this
Hilton hotel behind us," the guide went on, gesturing to her flock. "We will see parts of an old abbey
which makes up some of the building. This will be
followed by visiting a Jesuit college also."

"I'd rather visit a rest room and then see a cup of
coffee on one of those tables on the hotel patio," a
disgruntled matron was saying to her friend as they
passed Miranda. "We didn't need to visit those steam

baths earlier—all you have to do is walk down the block. Every stitch I'm wearing is sticking to me."

"It isn't the guide's fault that the bus isn't air-conditioned," her friend protested weakly as they followed the others.

"Sometimes I wonder whose side you're on . . ."

The acrimonious comment floated back to Miranda, who had remained by one of the columns as the others filed past. The suggestion about the patio table made her crane her neck and then smile as she discovered the patio restaurant of the hotel located just beyond the confines of the Bastion.

The restaurant was an attractive spot with rattan chairs set around tables decorated with hand-woven cloths and bright bouquets. As she made her way to it, a couple left a table near the edge of the enclosure and Miranda took possession gratefully. Every other table seemed to be taken, and even as she glanced around, she saw stragglers or outright deserters from the tour searching for a place to sit.

At that moment, a waiter approached for her order and she decided that tea and apple cake would do nicely as a substitute for lunch aboard the ship. When he left, she unzipped her purse and took out a brochure that she'd picked up from the purser's office on "Things to See" in Budapest. It was time, she decided, to really get to work. Shopping for china was all very well except that it couldn't occupy more than a short paragraph in her article—as Mitch would take great delight in pointing out.

"Hello . . . hello. What a pleasant surprise!" a feminine voice said.

Miranda looked up, to find Frieda beaming down at her.

"You will take pity on me, no?" the ship's hostess

asked, putting on a pathetic face. "If I don't have something cold this minute, I won't live to take you all on the evening tour." She flopped down in a chair at the other side of the table as Miranda said politely that she'd be glad of the company.

"Are you alone?" Frieda asked, her glance settling for a moment on the remaining empty chair at the table.

Miranda started to smile as she realized why the German girl was so anxious to share her space. "Why, yes," she replied, giving her a wide-eyed stare. "Quite alone. Were you expecting to see someone else?"

Frieda's plump shoulders moved in an uncaring shrug. "Is it so strange? When I saw you and Mitch on the other side of the river a bit earlier, you certainly seemed to be 'going steady.' Or do Americans use that phrase any longer?"

"I think it's a little dated these day," Miranda replied evasively. "Your English is so good, I wouldn't imagine you'd have any problems with American idioms."

"I don't." Frieda put out a hand to stop a passing waiter and said, "*Bier, bitte.*" The waiter gave her a reproving glance, but the hostess ignored it with Teutonic assurance, turning back to Miranda. "Languages are no problem for me. Besides, I lived in New York for a year and recently I've been dating an Englishman who works in Munich."

She broke off to search in her purse for a cigarette, giving Miranda a chance to study her more closely. At least she now had an explanation for the hostess's strange accent, which mixed tinges of the Bronx along with occasional Knightsbridge pronunciation. The ship's uniform she was wearing was nicely tailored, but Frieda's generous measurements put extra strain on the buttonholes. On the other hand, her dark beauty had a lush Rubenesque quality that was eye-catching, although Miranda doubted that she'd retain it in ten years' time.

Such thoughts apparently had occurred to Frieda, because she looked on enviously as the waiter deposited a generous piece of apple cake with whipped cream in front of Miranda and poured the tea. When they were alone again, she said, "It's been years since I could eat *schlag*—I mean whipped cream—without feeling guilty. I think you Americans have a different metabolism."

"I'll also have a different waistline if I keep on eating dessert for lunch."

"What does it matter? Apparently Mitch likes you the way you are. At least, that's how it looked to me on the Embankment." Frieda took a swallow from the glass of beer which had just been put in front of her. "I was surprised," she continued reflectively. "He didn't seem like the kind of man who'd show his feelings in public like that."

"You mean . . ."

". . . when he kissed you, of course. Now, if he'd been Italian—nothing would surprise me with them. Somehow I'd always suspected that Americans were like the English. Everything behind closed doors."

Miranda concentrated on taking her tea bag out of the pot at exactly that moment. She certainly couldn't tell Frieda that she'd only viewed a "show-and-tell" demonstration. It was probably better to let her think what she pleased. By the end of the trip, she wouldn't be in any doubt as to Mitch's true feelings.

"And speaking of closed doors . . ." Frieda was going on, forcing Miranda to pay attention again. "We were all wondering what went on behind yours yesterday." Seeing Miranda's perplexed look, she adopted a woman-of-the-world tone. "When Mitch wouldn't let anyone in your cabin. A person would have thought you were newlyweds."

"Why, that's absurd," Miranda replied, trying not to sound guilty. "I wasn't feeling too well when the doctor came, but afterward the stewardess . . ." Her voice trailed off as Frieda smiled in smug fashion and shook her head.

"The stewardess is a friend of mine and she told me that Mitch gave her explicit orders," Frieda announced. "Of course he was in and out during the afternoon, but she had to make sure that you didn't have any other visitors while she was on duty."

"But how could she do that?"

"The girls stay in the corridors when they're working—to be on call for passengers in the staterooms. And yesterday, Mitch was giving the orders." Frieda took a larger swallow of her beer and said, "It must be nice to have such a protective man. I've been looking for one all my life. Unfortunately, protection isn't what most of mine have in mind," she added bitterly.

There wasn't anything Miranda could say to help. It was difficult to even speak coherently, since Frieda's tale had sent her thoughts into orbit. At that moment, there wasn't any doubt in Miranda's mind about who'd undressed her after the doctor's visit. Her cheeks burned when she thought back and realized how Mitch had evaded the issue earlier. Not that it mattered, she told herself resignedly. Considering all her scrapes and bruises, he probably hadn't wasted any time tucking her under the covers out of sight.

"Isn't the cake to your liking?"

Frieda's voice penetrated Miranda's consciousness and she recovered enough to say, "It's fine. Why?"

"You looked as if you'd suddenly hit a sour apple."

"Not recently." Miranda took a sip of tea and determinedly changed the subject. "Is the nightclub tour going to be any good?"

The hostess shrugged. "It's something to do, and usually the passengers find it acceptable. Is Mitch taking you?"

Mitch again! Miranda wanted to scream as Frieda brought his name back into the conversation and, for the first time, could sympathize with his plight. Frieda was more than a clinging vine; she was a patch of poison ivy and it would take a determined male to escape. But as the brunette leaned forward and a button on her blouse popped free, Miranda reminded herself that most men would be quite happy if they didn't ever make it to freedom.

"You should be sitting inside the hotel where there's some air conditioning," Frieda said, giving Miranda a concerned look.

"What makes you say that?"

"Every time I ask you a question, you forget to answer. My English might not be so good, but it's not that bad."

Miranda smiled apologetically across the table at her. "Sorry. I have quite a few things on my mind."

"In that case, you shouldn't let him be wandering around Budapest alone. He's a lot of man to be on his own in this city."

Miranda sat up straighter. "That's ridiculous! I certainly don't have any hold on Mitch Emerson—I just work for him."

"I've been trying to find that kind of a job all my life," Frieda said, finishing the rest of her beer and then searching her purse for her wallet. "Unfortunately, the ones I've been offered in Munich don't have any long-range possibilities."

Miranda almost laughed aloud, wondering what Frieda would say if she confessed she'd be lucky to still be on Mitch's payroll by the end of the voyage. Instead she asked politely, "Are you going back to the ship now?"

Frieda nodded, finding some currency and putting it down on her check. "I'm on duty this afternoon until six and then I only have two hours off until I work the nightclub tour."

"It'll be nice to see a familiar face during the evening," Miranda said, finishing her tea and blotting her lips with the napkin. "Joe Miller's invited me to join him."

Frieda's eyebrows rose and then settled back into line. "He's all right—if you can ever find him without his mother. Maybe she's going along too."

"I doubt it." Miranda's tone was dry. "If you're returning to the ship now, shall we share a cab?"

"I'll be glad to." Frieda watched as Miranda handed a credit card to the hovering waiter and finally signed her bill. "I'm surprised that you don't want to go shopping in the square here."

"From what I could see, the booths just had embroidery and the usual gimcracks."

"You sound as if you're looking for something special," Frieda said as she got to her feet and led the way out of the restaurant toward the hotel taxi rank.

"I hoped to pick up some pieces of Herend china—that pattern with birds on it," Miranda confessed as they crossed a small cobblestone street. "Unfortunately, you have to buy a service for twelve or it's no dice."

"Not if you're interested in seconds," Frieda said, sounding like a brisk hostess again. "The government here doesn't publicize the practice, but there are some stores where you can find a bargain. There's a small one close by where the ship is docked. Come along, I'll show you."

The brunette hailed a taxi without further delay and made no attempt to indulge in small talk as they drove back across the river to the Pest side of the city. Miranda peered through the rear window to admire the spire of Matthias Church towering over the old Castle district before turning her attention ahead again.

Once the driver had turned down on a street which paralleled the Embankment, Frieda uttered a drawn-out sigh. "If we had any sense, we'd both be spending the day at Margaret Island. The swimming complex there is the best place in town to beat this humidity since no one can afford air conditioning." Her comment was accompanied by a gesture encompassing the interior, which was stifling despite air blowing through the open windows. She made an effort to smooth her hair, and added bitterly, "The only ones who gain anything by it are the owners of hairdressing salons."

A few minutes later, when the driver slowed at a traffic light near the *Donau*'s pier, Frieda addressed him sharply in a mixture of German and Hungarian. He pulled over to the curb in the middle of the block, barely missing a streetcar in the process.

Miranda reached for her wallet, but Frieda waved her aside. "Forget it, this goes on my expense account. I was doing a public-relations visit at the hotel before I met you in the restaurant."

"If you're sure . . ."

"Very sure." Frieda completed the financial transaction and motioned Miranda to accompany her as
she walked toward a small shop on the corner.

The temperature must have risen twenty degrees
since she'd started out in the morning, Miranda thought
as they trudged along the dusty sidewalk, past store-
fronts which look as if they'd been built in the thirties. Apparently there were apartments on upper floors
of the buildings, because pot plants decorated a few
of the iron balconies. Behind them, most windows
had blinds with broken slats, which gave them a
gap-toothed appearance. When combined with the
stained fronts of the old stone buildings, it made her
wish that she'd visited the city in earlier, grander
times. Even those scattered pots of flowers on the
balconies were a sad contrast to the literally hundreds
of window boxes blazing with color in Munich's main
square, which she'd seen earlier in the week.

"It'll be good to get back on the ship and take a
shower," Frieda muttered, blotting her cheeks with
the back of her hand. "After that, I don't plan to set
foot ashore until the nightclub tour."

"Perhaps by then the temperature will be more
bearable," Miranda replied, wondering if she still had
determination enough to wander around the Parliament Building before dinner. She pulled up beside
Frieda when they reached the tiny corner shop and
stared in the small display windows. The glass could
have profited by washing, and it was difficult to see
the dim, unlighted interior. There certainly wasn't
any attempt at attractive arrangements in the windows; apparently the owners merely shoved in the
most convenient items at hand to let passersby know
what they stocked. Miranda saw two radios—the
kind teenagers carry down the sidewalk with rock

music blasting from the speakers—next to three pack-
ages of powdered detergent. Another corner was filled
with plastic bags of hard candy and a grimy card
displaying pocket combs. She shook her head, discouraged by it all, when Frieda indicated a shelf at
the rear holding odd pieces of china. "There's some
Herend—probably seconds. Make sure the price is
okay. There's apt to be a sliding scale in places like
this."

"Are you going in?" Miranda asked hopefully. "My
Hungarian is limited to '*kavet*' and '*A tobbi a magae.*' "

Frieda gave her a pitying look. "You won't get far
with 'coffee' and 'keep the change.' "

"At least it's better than my Russian. All I know of
that is 'I love you' and 'good-bye.' Languages aren't
really my thing," she added, searching through her
purse. "I have a phrase book in here somewhere."

Frieda uttered a snort and reached for the door. "But
you don't want to find a policeman and they don't
care if the pen of your aunt is red. Come along.
Maybe I'll find a piece of Herend myself. I should
take a few knickknacks home on this trip."

Miranda grinned and urged Frieda ahead of her.
"Thanks a million. I promise to write a letter to your
bosses saying what a terrific job you did on the
cruise."

"You might put in a good word with Mitch while
you're doing it," Frieda said, smiling back. Then her
expression changed as a young girl behind the counter
evidently asked what they wanted. Frieda replied in
a language that Miranda didn't understand, but passed
muster with the clerk, because the girl gestured
toward a niche behind the counter where a few more
odd pieces of china were displayed.

Frieda asked another question and almost reluctantly the girl reached back to place the Herend on the counter in front of them. At that moment, the shop door opened again and the clerk's face brightened as she recognized a familiar customer. She muttered something to Frieda and walked to the front of the shop to wait on the newcomer.

"She doesn't seem very eager to sell us anything," Miranda murmured as she picked up a saucer and then a cup which didn't match it.

"That's what happens when there's no competition." Frieda inspected one of the pieces and put it down again. "Not much in this lot, is there?"

"Not really." Miranda's tone was regretful, since it was apparently the closest she was going to come to achieving her objective. Her glance searched the display cabinets and shelves, which seemed more for storage than anything else. She was about to suggest giving the whole thing up as a bad idea when she sighted two bud vases with the popular bird pattern at the back of the counter, almost hidden by a stack of packing material. "I think we've hit the jackpot," she told Frieda elatedly as she stretched across the counter and pulled them out of hiding.

They were two charming pieces of white porcelain featuring the hand-painted pattern decor which contributed to Herend's popularity in the world market. Although only five or six inches high, their exaggerated bulbous bases and narrow necks gave them an old-world appearance which was distinctly different.

Miranda smiled when she realized that the silhouette was almost a carbon copy of onion church spires she'd admired along the Danube's shores at the start of their cruise. Except for the decoration, she decided as she picked up one of the vases to admire the pattern of tiny colorful birds perched on a branch.

And even the bright gold church domes didn't boast the delightful butterflies and whimsical insects which appeared in a random design over the rest of the glazed surface.

"They're certainly unique," Frieda said, comparing its matching companion carefully. "Unfortunately, the neck is so narrow, you couldn't put more than one flower stem in it at a time."

"Maybe they're not very practical, but they surely have a lot of appeal," Miranda replied, refusing to be discouraged. "Almost Victorian—wouldn't you say? And the quality can't be faulted, especially if it's a second."

"Umm. I see what you mean." Frieda ran her finger over the porcelain and nodded approvingly. "It seems all right. I'm not enough of an expert to judge the decoration."

"This one looks fine to me," Miranda said, delighted by her discovery. "Besides, I don't want to put it on exhibition—I just want to use it for roses now and then." She looked inquiringly at Frieda. "Are you going to buy the other?"

"I might as well. If they don't get carried away with their profit margin."

"At least you can haggle in their language."

"I intend to." Frieda looked impatiently across the shop to where the young clerk was gossiping with the other customer, oblivious of her duties. The hostess snapped out something that made her pause and stare across at them, obviously annoyed to be interrupted.

There didn't seem to be any real disagreement in the words that followed, Miranda thought, listening to the exchange. The girl took her time about coming over, but only bestowed a casual glance on the vases before naming a price.

Frieda nodded, saying to Miranda in a low voice, "It's all right. I'll pay. Put some of that wrapping paper around them before she changes her mind."

Miranda nodded, her eyes sparkling at the thought of a bargain, and hurriedly wrapped Frieda's vase in a thick wad of paper. She fastened it with cellophane tape and then, since the financial transaction was completed, said brightly to the salesgirl, "I won't bother to wrap mine—it can just go in my purse. I'll carry it carefully," she said, tucking it into her shoulder bag.

"Then let's go," Frieda said in an undertone after another glance at the clerk, who was frowning at the barrage of English. "It looks as if she's having second thoughts about the whole business."

"Maybe she didn't charge enough."

"It's not our fault if she doesn't know her stock," Frieda said, opening the shop door and ushering Miranda out into the street when the clerk suddenly disappeared into the back of the shop through another door. "Remember the saying about 'all's fair in love and war.' "

"I'm not sure that holds true for Herend china," Miranda replied as they started across to the quay on the other side, where the *Donau* could be seen.

At that moment, a car pulled up along the curb in front of them and the Millers climbed out, lingering only long enough to speak to their driver before heading for the ship's gangway. Miranda decided that she didn't really want to discuss her day in Budapest before they met at the dinner table, and turned to Frieda on an impulse. "I think I'll do a little more window-shopping before I get on board," she said. "You go ahead."

Frieda's expression showed that she really couldn't

find any attraction in tramping around the city's dusty streets. "Whatever you say. I'll see you out on the quay when we gather for the nightclub tour, if not before."

"All right. Thanks again for bargaining in the shop."

"It was easy." Frieda smiled and clutched her unwieldy bundle carefully. "It'll be a miracle if I get it home without breaking it." She waved and hurried on across the street during a lull in the traffic.

Miranda didn't wait to see her progress. When she'd noticed the Millers' car pulling up, she also thought she'd caught a glimpse of a tall, dark-haired figure at the rail of the ship. She'd felt mildly reluctant to join the Millers, but the thought of an early reunion with her employer was appalling. Her feelings hadn't changed since that tempestuous leave-taking and she was even considering skipping dinner so she could escape on the nightclub tour without coming under Mitch's critical eye.

Probably that wasn't possible, she told herself as she rounded the corner and set off aimlessly down another dusty street. She *could* postpone their meeting, though, even if it meant risking sore feet and exhaustion in the process.

She managed to waste another two hours by looking in shop windows and sitting on benches, content to watch the people going by and observe the sporadic river traffic. Despite the big-city noises, the mood of Budapest seemed to match her own—a surface normality with underlying unhappiness. The city fathers had obviously tried to make their mark in the modern world with the new hotels to woo the tourists, but the effect was overshadowed by the decaying grandeur of the past.

Miranda rose from her bench after that conclusion,

deciding that the heat was making her morbid. Better to go back to the ship and try the therapeutic effects of a nice long shower.

She was delighted to find that there were no familiar faces at the gangway when she went up it a little later. Even the vestibule in front of the purser's office which was usually crowded was completely deserted. The sound of voices came from behind a closed door nearby—probably a staff meeting, she decided.

Even the corridor was empty, and she smiled as she unlocked her stateroom door and slipped inside, carefully securing it behind her. After that, it only took a few minutes to shed her clothes and make her way under the shower.

She was about to turn off the water five minutes later when a knocking on her cabin door made her give a start of surprise. It was repeated even more loudly as she shut off the shower and pushed back the soaking curtain. "I'm coming—" she began, breaking off as she heard the sound of a key in the lock and then the opening door, brought up short by the chain she'd fastened on it.

"What's going on out there?" she called, stepping across to open the bathroom door. She remembered belatedly that she wasn't in any condition for visitors and quickly closed it again, leaving just enough room to stick her shower-capped head around the edge. "You!" she accused as she met Mitch's piercing glare from the corridor. "What in the devil do you think you're doing?"

"If you can bring yourself to take the hardware off this damned thing"—he gave the bottom of the door a kick to emphasize his words—"I'll be happy to tell you."

"But I'm just out of the shower." Miranda became

aware that she was on the defensive again and tried to shift tactics. "Besides, you don't have any right to come blasting into my cabin without an invitation." Her tone lowered as she noticed two passengers peering over his shoulder as they tried to get past him in the corridor. It was evident that she and Mitch were going to be a main topic of conversation during dinner.

Mitch looked behind him and his expression turned even stonier, showing that he wasn't unaware of this latest development. "I'd like to discuss our business now," he said with a *pas-devant-les-domestiques* glare that didn't need translating.

The combination was too much for Miranda. "Give me a minute," she mumbled, and felt like a turtle as she pulled her head back in, away from curious eyes.

It took just a few seconds to grab her short toweling robe and put it on, belting it securely. Only then did she open the door and reach for the chain which was keeping Mitch out.

He didn't waste any time coming in the stateroom, ignoring the couple who still hovered in the hallway, ostensibly intrigued by a poster of Vienna's Schönbrunn Palace tacked up on the wall to help sell shore excursions.

"Damned busybodies," Mitch muttered, closing the door with a slam. "You'd think they'd have something else to do."

"I don't see why. Watching you try to break down a cabin door is certainly more exciting than a happy hour in the main lounge," Miranda said coolly.

"That just goes to show that you haven't kept up with the latest events. Our happy hour today came complete with a victim, stretcher, and ambulance. Right now, most of the passenger list is up there drinking heavily to make up for the shock." He walked on in the stateroom, giving it a cursory glance before pushing aside a pillow and sitting down on the divan under the porthole. "I gather that you missed all the excitement."

"Good Lord! No wonder it was like a morgue when I came aboard," Miranda said, and then grimaced. "I hope that was a poor choice of words."

"Frieda would think so. A twisted ankle isn't usually fatal."

"Frieda! You mean she was . . ."

"The victim?" He nodded and leaned back, trying to make himself comfortable on a mattress that wasn't overly endowed with springs. " 'Fraid so."

"Then it happened after she came back aboard." Miranda sank down on the other couch and frowned as she thought about it. "At least she looked fine when I left her a while ago."

"Where was that?"

"The other side of the street." She gestured vaguely beyond the porthole. "We'd been shopping in that sort of dumpy place on the corner. Then Frieda had to get back aboard to prepare for the nightclub tour."

"And you?"

For the first time, the determined undertone in his voice penetrated. "I decided to walk around a little more," she said defensively. "What's wrong with that?"

There was a pause. Then he drawled, "Not a thing. Probably it was one of the smarter moves you've made today."

"I don't understand." Her voice rose, showing that her newfound poise was slipping under his intent regard. "Surely nobody attacked Frieda aboard ship—in front of half the passenger list."

He grimaced wryly. "What is it about the feminine

mind that allows it to go straight to the point—ignoring any logical pitfalls that might prove dangerous?"

Miranda stirred uneasily, determined not to get involved in another battle of words that she knew she'd lose. "Now, look, you didn't break in here to—"

"I didn't break in at all," he interrupted. "Actually it was an errand of mercy."

"—break in here," Miranda continued inexorably, ignoring his defense, "simply to start a stupid philosophic discussion about female stereotypes."

"You're improving by the day."

"Maybe you'd do me a favor and get to the point before I freeze to death in this robe."

As soon as her words were out, Miranda regretted them, because Mitch obligingly turned his attention to the abbreviated clothing in question, letting his glance linger overlong on her expanse of bare legs. Her annoyance rose when he merely said, "It looks as if those scratches are healing okay."

"I feel fine." She rose to her feet and gave the belt of her robe a vicious twitch. "Now, if you don't mind—I'd like to dress for dinner."

"Feel free," he said, not moving an inch. "I gather that you're still going on this nightclub excursion?"

"Why, yes. Unless Frieda's accident washed out the evening." Miranda decided suddenly that her curiosity outweighed her irritation and she sat down on the edge of her bed again. "Would you please tell me what happened?"

"I knew that you'd get around to the proper . . ." He broke off as her lips thinned. "Okay. Frieda tripped on a cord—one of those that the musicians use for their speakers—when she was dragging a microphone around. She wears those damned high heels and the dance floor was slippery. Even then, everything would have been all right except that she banged her head on the edge of a table as she fell. That's what knocked her out, I guess."

"It doesn't sound suspicious," Miranda said slowly as the silence lengthened between them.

"It wasn't. There was a crowd around. Joe Miller was helping her move the platform she uses. So was the major. As a matter of fact," Mitch said wryly, "so was I."

"She'll be all right though, won't she?"

"I should think so." Mitch drew a deep breath and then continued. "That wasn't what bothered me. At least, not really."

It was one of the few times that Miranda had seen his assurance crack and she wouldn't have been normal if she hadn't felt a surge of satisfaction.

He must have noticed her expression, because he went on gruffly, "Gerhard—the purser," he explained, as she looked puzzled for a minute, "thought Frieda should have some of her belongings when they took her to the hospital. In case she had to stay overnight."

"That makes sense."

He nodded. "Anyhow, he decided he should stay with her, so he gave me his passkey and asked me to find a stewardess to get some stuff from her stateroom. Which would have been fine," he went on, "except there weren't any stewardesses around. Naturally. There never are when you need one."

"Like looking for a policeman," Miranda agreed.

"So I used the passkey," Mitch added glumly, "and went in to pack an overnight case for her. And what do you know—the lousy stateroom had been ransacked to a fare-thee-well. Her belongings were strewn all over the place."

Miranda inhaled sharply. "My Lord, why?"

"Damned if I know. Anyhow, I grabbed some of the things she'd need and put them in a zipper bag for Gerhard to send with her—making sure I locked the cabin door behind me. But after I'd delivered the bag, I thought maybe this deal was connected with your troubles at Durnstein, so I . . ."

". . . came thumping on my door." She smiled at him tremulously. "I'm glad you did, but thank heavens it was a false alarm."

Mitch thoughtfully rubbed the back of his thumb against his lower lip. "I hope you're right, but I'm not sure about that."

"But nothing's happened to me and nobody came calling this time." She gestured around at her orderly stateroom, which showed only the usual signs of occupancy, with her purse on the dressing table and a pile of reference pamphlets stacked near the closed-circuit TV.

"On the other hand, you were with Frieda just before she came back aboard ship."

"So were lots of other people. I met her in a café by the Fishermen's Bastion and half the tourists in Budapest must have been around the place. We just shared a cab on the way back because it was convenient."

"Okay." He massaged the side of his neck and then got to his feet wearily. "At least Gerhard will tell the captain to increase security while we're here."

Miranda watched him move to the stateroom door. "Frieda could have been involved in smuggling or something like that. As a crew member making regular port calls, she'd have plenty of opportunities." Her voice dropped as he turned to face her, leaning against the door as if he needed the support. "What's the matter? You look beat."

"I'm fine. It's just been a long day." He reached for the knob and pulled the door ajar. "I'll see you around." He hesitated as if he had something else on his mind, and then obviously decided against it—giving her a terse nod before going out in the corridor and closing the stateroom door firmly behind him.

His departure should have made Miranda feel better, since she'd emerged relatively unscathed. Therefore, it didn't make any sense that she sank back against the pillows on the divan, suddenly as exhausted as a long-distance runner, but without any of the exhilaration of a winning finish. She would have given a great deal if Mitch had postponed his departure for another half-minute—long enough to mention what was really on his mind. That look he'd given her had been enough to make her pulse start bounding like a wild thing—which wasn't logical at all.

Miranda glanced up to see her reflection in the mirror over the dressing table and shook her head sadly. Somehow by the time she emerged for the nightclub tour she'd need to put a better face on things, literally and figuratively. She'd also have to learn to face reality in the days ahead—a reality which certainly wouldn't have Mitch Emerson in it once her cruise on the *Donau* was finished.

7

It was considerably later before Miranda had to test her newfound determination.

She was just going to open her stateroom door when a soft knocking sounded.

She frowned and put her head close to the wood. "Who is it?"

"It's me—Joe," came Joe Miller's slightly aggrieved tone.

"Oh, of course." Miranda pulled open the door and flashed him an apologetic smile. "Am I late? I thought I'd meet you on the dock."

Joe's expression lightened as he surveyed her. "No, you're right on time. I just didn't know if you were coming—since you missed dinner and everything."

"I'm sorry about that." She gave him her jacket so he could help her on with it before they left the corridor. "Actually I wasn't hungry, so I had my stewardess bring me some soup." It wasn't exactly the truth, but Miranda didn't intend to confess that she hadn't felt up to another long meal and having to make polite conversation.

"You're feeling okay, aren't you?" Before she could answer, he patted her shoulder reassuringly. "You must be, because you look great. I like that outfit."

Miranda smiled her thanks, only partially convinced

by his compliment. Her coral-and-white cotton knit wasn't what she would have chosen for a nightclub visit in town, but it fitted nicely, with a low boat neckline, and the separate jacket added a dressy touch. Besides, as Joe probably realized, her travel wardrobe was limited. Or maybe he didn't realize it, she thought after another glance at him. His white shirt gleamed under a silk suit woven in a beige-and-burgundy plaid. Sleek Italian loafers of cordovan leather completed the ensemble. For an instant she was tempted to ask him how much luggage he'd brought with him and then sensibly dismissed the idea. He was a pleasant shipboard acquaintance and they merely had to coexist for a few more days.

Joe caught her elbow in a protective grip as they made their way across the gangway, and he didn't bother to release her when they reached the dock. Instead, he tightened his clasp as they strolled up the stairs toward the group of passengers clustered beside the street. "I've been looking forward to this all day," he said, bending his head to whisper in her ear. "My God, it'll be nice to do something that I want to do—just for a change."

"I saw you and your mother driving off this morning—coming back, too," Miranda told him, trying unobtrusively to put a little more space between them. "Didn't she want to celebrate tonight?"

His eyebrows shot up. "You have to be kidding. Visiting a nightclub isn't in her scheme of things. She decided to have an early night after driving around in the heat all day. I'm glad it's finally cooled off a little—" He broke off when they came to the rest of the group, in time to hear one of the purser's assistants exhorting the group to "Follow me, please. We walk to the club. Much easier than taking a bus."

"And cheaper for them, too," Joe said cynically. "Do you mind?"

"Heavens, no." Miranda stuck out a foot, exhibiting a neat soft leather espadrille. "I'm set for anything—walking shoes and my trusty purse with traveler's checks," she added, adjusting the strap of her shoulder bag. "It's par for the course, day and night."

He shrugged and looked both ways before they started across the almost deserted street. "Some of the crew told me that this nightclub is third-rate anyhow, so it doesn't matter what kind of an impression we make."

Miranda felt a letdown at his words, although she wasn't surprised. "Did Frieda say that?"

"Actually it was that brunette in the purser's office," Joe said, deliberately slowing his pace so there was an appreciable distance between them and the rest of the passengers. "She waited until Gerhard was out of hearing, though." He tilted his head to look down at Miranda. "I suppose you've learned the news about Frieda?"

"Her accident?" About to announce that Mitch had told her, Miranda had second thoughts and merely nodded.

"It was rotten luck," Joe said, sending a small stone on the sidewalk flying with a well-aimed kick. "She would merely have ended up with a twisted ankle if she hadn't hit her head on that damned table on the way down." He grimaced, remembering. "The worst part was that we all just stood around and watched."

Miranda crossed her fingers in her jacket pocket. "I didn't know that you saw the whole thing."

"So did your friend Mitch, and a couple other fellows. Frieda likes to corral any available men on

the passenger list," he commented. "Not that any of
us objected. It was part of her job and she didn't try
to pretend anything else." Joe absently tightened his
grip on Miranda's elbow when they came to another
deserted street, and then dropped it to gesture around
him as they crossed. "It's hard to believe we're in the
middle of the city, isn't it? They may not roll up the
sidewalks, but they're certainly deserted, and if anybody lives in these apartment houses, they don't
waste any money on electricity."

"I was wondering why they closed the shutters in
this season," Miranda mused, glancing up at the
shadowed buildings. "It's the only time they'd get
any cool air." She shivered suddenly as she thought
about the desolate surroundings. "Maybe we should
catch up with the rest of the tour."

"Relax," Joe said, laughing as he pulled her closer.
"Nothing's going to happen tonight. This is still a
fairly respectable part of town. That's why Frieda
chose the nightclub. Plus the fact that the entertain-
ment was cheap. Europeans don't miss any way to
make a fast buck. They'd have you believe that money-
grubbing is an American trait, but they're the ones
who invented the game. It's smart to count your
fingers after you count your change."

Miranda's eyebrows went up at his vehement
tone. "You sound bitter. Not a bit like the easygoing
Southerner I met on the bus. What happened? Did
someone give you a bad time today?"

"What makes you think that?" he asked suspiciously.

"Oh, Lord—nothing special," she said, wishing
that she'd concentrated on the weather or the service
aboard the *Donau*. "I guess I was just surprised. My
day was so bland that I might as well have been at
home."

Joe's expression eased. "What did you do?"

"The usual. I walked around, window-shopped, and decided I wouldn't ever wear an embroidered peasant blouse after I got it home. Frieda and I had tea together at the Fishermen's Bastion."

"She didn't mention it when I saw her in the lounge."

"I'm not surprised. We merely shared a table and then a taxi back to the ship. Hey—that must be the nightclub," she added, pointing to a canopied doorway in the middle of the block, where the tour group was disappearing. "I guess it doesn't rate a doorman."

Joe gave a snort of laughter. "Hardly. I've only seen four cars since we left the ship tonight." As they neared the doorway he said, "They might do better to spend their money on a new canopy. That one looks as if it's been around since the Romans."

Miranda bestowed an appraising glance on the tattered canvas fringe. "At least since Attila the Hun hit town."

"Let's hope the floor show isn't of the same vintage," Joe muttered, pushing open a glass door.

Once inside, they stopped to adjust to the shadowed surroundings. There was a bar of sorts along the wall to their left, where most of the regular customers were nursing drinks and appeared deep in conversation. The center of the room was cleared for a stage with a raised platform at the back where three musicians were leisurely sorting through their music and a stagehand was trying to improve the drape of a red velour curtain which was stained on the edge.

The tour group had been led to tables at the back of the room and was being sandwiched into them by two waiters who ignored all protests.

"It looks like an obedience class at a dog show,"

Miranda said, caught up with giggles when a waiter pointed to two vacant chairs and the remaining two passengers from the group subsided reluctantly into them.

"Notice the language barrier that's suddenly been erected," Joe said, watching the performance. When some of the comments carried across the floor, he grinned. "It's just as well that neither side can understand, or there'd be a riot."

"Things should calm down soon," Miranda said, seeing another waiter carrying a loaded tray toward the tables. "There goes the red and white wine."

"If you want anything else, you pay extra. I've been on these jaunts before." Joe was searching for an available seat as a stagehand at the edge of the curtain started lowering the lights. "Looks as if we're destined for the back row—unless you want to skip the whole thing. We could look for another place to have a drink."

Remembrance of the empty, shadowed streets made Miranda decide that there was safety in numbers. Joe might not like being part of the group, but right then, she decided it was the best place to be. "I'd hate to miss the floor show," she told him over her shoulder as she started for the back of the club. "Don't forget, this is all new to me."

He clearly wasn't pleased by her sudden show of enthusiasm, but he obediently trailed behind her and settled into the last available seat.

Without comment, a passing waiter deposited two glasses of red wine and two of white in front of them. Then, seeing Joe's annoyed expression, he also put down a carafe of the red wine in the center of the table.

Miranda nodded her thanks and took a sip from

the nearest glass. She didn't choke on it, but only because it had been a very small sip and she put the glass back down hastily.

By then, the stagehand had darkened most of the lights except for a white spot at the wings, but Joe must have been watching her more carefully than she'd thought.

"If you drink both of those," he said, jerking a thumb toward her two wineglasses, "you'll have a hangover tomorrow that won't quit."

"But I understood that Hungarian Tokay was famous," she replied, bewildered.

"You don't think they're going to ladle the good stuff out for free, do you?" He stopped a waiter by simply clutching his coat sleeve. "What would you really like, Miranda?"

"How about tonic water?"

"And I'll have a beer." When the waiter started to protest, Joe pulled out his wallet and shoved a bill in his hand. "Keep it coming."

The waiter nodded and disappeared. Miranda muttered, "I thought he didn't understand English," and then subsided as the musicians on the platform suddenly blasted out an introduction for the master of ceremonies.

It was a half-hour later before the lights came up again—long enough for a short intermission. At least that's what the master of ceremonies announced with a smirk before the spotlight disappeared and the musicians did the same thing.

Joe shifted on his chair, obviously trying to get comfortable. "Well, what do you think of it?" he asked Miranda.

She shook her head, bemused. "It's the darnedest thing. The whole show's like a time capsule from the thirties. Did you notice the shabby shoes on that chorus line? And the costumes!"

"I'm not complaining about them," Joe replied in an arch tone.

"Well, they didn't waste any material," Miranda agreed. "But considering the measurements of the dancers—"

"A little more camouflage wouldn't have been a bad idea." Then he shook his head. "I must be getting old."

"Just discriminating." Miranda surveyed the room, noting that the heavy red curtains had seen better days, as had the tables and chairs. "I guess I expected something different. Gypsy violins or dancers—not a worn-out chorus line and tired American songs."

"You mean you didn't like that tenor?"

"If he was a 'phenomenal success from Hollywood,' the movie industry's in worse shape than I've heard."

"The closest he's been to Hollywood is the other bank of the Danube," Joe said, raising a finger to catch their waiter's eye and then pointing at his empty beer glass. "Sure you don't want to join me?" he asked Miranda who was idly tracing patterns on the side of her glass of tonic water. "The beer's not bad."

"No, thanks. This is fine." She observed the rest of their group, who seemed determined to finish all the wine that was put in front of them. "Everybody's enjoying the night out."

"Some people like to watch the test pattern on television, too." Joe leaned back to let the waiter deposit a new glass of beer in front of him. "Mother had the right idea."

"What's that?"

"She said I should take you to one of the hotels on the Embankment or stay aboard and relax in the lounge. Although after what happened there . . ." He shrugged and let his voice drop.

"You mean Frieda?" Miranda chewed on her lip as she thought about it. "I wonder how she's doing."

"Who knows?" Joe sat up straighter as he gazed toward the door. "Maybe there's the person we should ask."

Miranda followed his glance. "Mitch! For heaven's sake!"

Joe gave her a sideways look. "Didn't you know he was coming here?"

"I can't remember," Miranda stalled, as she watched her employer ingratiate himself with the patrons at the bar—an attractive redhead in particular.

"She's better-looking than anything in the chorus line," Joe observed, showing that his attention was focused in the same place. "I wonder if they're old friends."

"You could always go over and ask him. He might even be generous and introduce you to the lady."

Joe grinned at the bitterness in her tone. "Not tonight, thanks. This is one time I'm not interested in switching partners, and if that boss of yours wanders over here, I won't hesitate to tell him."

"You don't have to worry. From the look of things, he's going to help the redhead prop up the bar," Miranda said, trying to sound as if she didn't care. Inwardly, she was surprised how even the emergence of Mitch in the same room set her nerve ends tingling. Undoubtedly, she'd have the same re-action, she told herself severely, if she landed next to a patch of ragweed in hay-fever season.

"Want to change your drink?"

Joe's question finally trickled through her consciousness and she blinked as she looked sideways. "What for?" she asked blankly.

"Because you looked as if it suddenly had a bad taste. We don't have to stay for the rest of the program. We could wander around—maybe stroll along the Embankment and look for a place to have a drink that offers a little privacy. It would be nice to get to know you better," he added, leaning close and brushing his lips over her cheek in a soft caress.

Miranda's first instinct was to pull back. She might have made it a gradual move if a familiar masculine voice hadn't shattered the silence at that moment. "I can see you're enjoying the show," Mitch said, materializing at her elbow like a genie out of a bottle.

His sudden appearance made Miranda jump. That set the rickety table rocking and she almost had a lapful of tonic water before Mitch reached out a hand to prevent it. He shook his head as Joe straggled reluctantly to his feet. "Don't get up—I can't stay."

"You mean you have other plans?" Miranda said, directing a baleful look toward the redhead.

Mitch's mouth quirked as he admitted, "Something like that. A friend of a friend." He turned to Joe. "I just wanted to remind Miranda to have an early night. I expect her to be all set when we go to Szentendre tomorrow morning."

The way he talked over her head made Miranda want to give him a swift kick in the shins. Her thoughts must have filtered through to him, because he took a step backward then and nodded casually. "Looks as if the show's about to start. See you later."

Joe muttered something under his breath which sounded like "Not if I have anything to say about it." Miranda couldn't confirm it, because the music suddenly reverberated in their ears. Possibly the combo had decided that the remainder of the show would go over better if the audience was reduced to a state of shock. Joe's lips were moving, but Miranda could only shake her head. He nodded grimly and took a sizable gulp of his drink as the chorus line burst onto the scene again.

Miranda tried to ignore the women's laddered black stockings and molting maribou boas during the opening number. It would have been a relief if she could have lost herself in the show, because her glance traitorously veered from time to time to the bar area. The view of the redhead clinging like a limpet to Mitch's arm didn't improve her evening and it was small solace that Mitch himself appeared engrossed in the floor show rather than his companion.

He caught Miranda in her observation at that moment and she could see his amusement. Her head snapped back to the chorus line so fast that a muscle in her neck protested and she said, "Damn, damn, damn," with increasing violence.

It was unfortunate that her comment cut through the still air just an instant after the music had finished and before the audience stirred themselves to apathetic applause. Heads swiveled eagerly as the tour group wondered if they'd been watching the wrong show.

"Really, my dear," Joe reproved, drawing back in his chair fastidiously.

Miranda ground her teeth together, while the audience waited for something else to happen and then reluctantly shifted their attention to the stage again.

"I didn't think it was *that* bad," Joe went on in an undertone. "You have to make allowances for their budget, after all. I suppose any kind of talent comes high these days."

"I didn't mean . . . I wasn't talking about. . . ." Miranda's explanation faltered under his reproachful expression. She heard the master of ceremonies say something in broken English about a magician, and she gestured toward the stage. "Oh, great! I really like this kind of an act," she said, trying to sound enthusiastic. "Maybe they're saving the best for the last."

The magician's talent was certainly of higher caliber than the opening acts, and even the baritone who closed the show was pleasantly entertaining. Miranda joined in the applause as the cast took their bows and then turned a smiling face to Joe. "I really had a fine time," she told him, reaching for her purse.

"Then I wonder why you're in such a hurry to leave?" He let the silence lengthen between them before he took pity on her and grinned. "I'm just giving you a bad time. The show wasn't so bad that we should demand our money back, but that's about all you could say for it. And the atmosphere certainly isn't inspiring, so we might as well sample some other place." He pushed back his chair after tossing another bill on the table for a tip.

"We're not the only ones with that idea," Miranda commented when they had to queue up behind the other passengers who had headed for the door. "This reminds me of a Monopoly game. Go straight to jail—do not pass Go and don't collect two hundred dollars on the way."

Joe nodded. "One thing for sure—they'd have to pay me two hundred dollars to sit through that show again." His glance was combing the bar patrons as he spoke. "Apparently Mitch and the redhead got out early."

That disclosure didn't improve Miranda's mood, but she kept a noncommittal expression on her face as they approached the door of the nightclub and nodded to the waiter who was holding it open for them.

She'd started to follow the other members of the tour, when Joe urged her toward the curb and pulled her to a stop. "There's no point in following the flock—let's cut off here to the right and see if we can pick up a taxi."

"I hate to act the heavy employer," came a familiar voice behind them, "but Miranda had better get back to the ship and try for a decent night's sleep. If she's really sincere about wanting a permanent job on the magazine."

"Of course I'm sincere," Miranda said, her voice more breathless than she'd hoped. She held Mitch's glance firmly, however, as he lingered beside them. "We thought you'd gone ahead."

"It seemed like a good idea to keep an eye on you," he said blandly before turning to Joe. "I'll be glad to escort Miranda back to the ship—if you'd rather check out the nightlife at one of the hotels."

"That won't be necessary" Joe spit the words out— obviously finding it hard to keep his tone civil. "*I'll* walk Miranda back to the ship, since I asked her out for the evening. Now, if you'll excuse us . . ."

Mitch merely gestured them ahead of him, but Miranda thought there was a complacent look about him before Joe marched her up the sidewalk in double time, muttering something under his breath as they widened the gap between them. Miranda only caught a word or two, but it didn't bear repeating and she pretended to be engrossed in the window display of a home-furnishings store they were passing.

Joe evidently realized that his behavior wasn't exemplary, because he caught her hand and squeezed it. "Sorry. I wasn't keen on chaperons fifteen years ago and I sure as hell could do without one now."

Miranda shot a quick glance behind them. "He isn't very close. As a matter of fact, he's bringing up the rear with that girl from the purser's office." She turned to face the front again, adding bitterly, "Some chaperon."

"I suppose he'd trail us if we tried to duck off down one of these blocks," Joe groused as they reached another deserted intersection. "If he's this much of a watchdog with everybody that works for him, it's a wonder that he has any employees left."

The same thought had occurred to Miranda and she made a mental note to check it out with her cousin when she got back to New York. *If* she ever did, she thought a moment or two later, when a cyclist riding without lights careened through the intersection, almost shaving material off the back of her skirt before she could reach the sidewalk.

"Damned fool!" Joe said angrily when the rider's laughter floated back to them. He glanced apologetically down into her pale features. "I'm sorry about that—I didn't see him. You weren't hurt, were you?"

"No, I'm fine," Miranda said, not lingering near the curb. "And it wasn't your fault. You were in the line of fire too. I thought taxi drivers were the only people to guard against here."

"That kind seem to be all over the world," Joe said, sounding resigned. "This just isn't our night."

"Probably because we forgot to check our biorhythms before we started out," she said, trying to lighten his mood.

"Mmm." Joe's quick glance over his shoulder showed that he placed most of the blame elsewhere, but he didn't bother to contradict her

They strolled on in silence for the rest of the trip to the Embankment and the quay. The tour group had broken up into couples or foursomes and occasionally a burst of conversation could be heard, but for the most part it was a subdued walk. Miranda wanted to check and see if Mitch were bringing up the rear but refused to let him know that she was curious.

A check of her watch showed that it was just after midnight, but the darkened buildings and streets around them made it seem much later. She tried to visualize London or midtown Manhattan at the same hour, and shook her head—there simply was no comparison.

The parked cars near the quay where the *Donau* was tied up had disappeared while they'd been away, with the exception of one, and that driver was slouched behind the wheel as if he'd had a long wait.

"There must be some VIP aboard," Miranda said to Joe as they started across the street.

"What makes you think so?"

She gestured toward the car. "Well, it isn't a taxi, so he must be waiting for someone. And I doubt if it belongs to a visitor on that Romanian boat tied up beyond us. Theirs is strictly a low-budget operation, from the looks of things."

Joe frowned as he surveyed the scene under the streetlight at the edge of the pier. "You might be right. It's hardly worth wasting any sleep on, is it?"

Miranda opened her mouth to say that she was just

making conversation, but decided against it. She couldn't blame him for being testy, considering the way the evening had turned out.

Once they crossed the gangway and reached the confines of the lower deck, she thought he'd automatically steer them up the stairs toward the lounge. Instead, Joe gave her a perfunctory smile, saying, "I'll let you get off to your downy couch. I'd hate to jeopardize your job, and if we went to the lounge, Mitch would be occupying the bar stool next to us—breathing down our necks." He put a hand under her chin and tilted her head back to drop a light kiss on her lips. "We'll do it another time when the ground rules are different. I'll see you at breakfast, love." He gave her a gentle shove down the corridor toward her stateroom.

Definitely a "here's-your-hat—what's-your-hurry" move, Miranda decided with a wry smile as she closed her stateroom door behind her a minute or so later. It wasn't surprising under the circumstances. Taking everything into account, she felt that Joe would concentrate on more accessible females for the rest of the voyage.

She dropped her purse on the bureau, happy to finally dispose of the heavy thing. Before she left on the trip in the morning, she'd have to see if she could lighten the load.

She kicked off her shoes with a sigh and walked into the bathroom to undress, pulling on a thigh-length nylon travel robe over a shortie nightgown. As she went back into the stateroom, she remembered that her porthole overlooked the quay, which meant that she'd better make sure that the drapes were securely closed or she'd be providing a floor show for the loungers along the Embankment. She glanced idly out toward the street as she knelt on the divan to pull the drape, but remained motionless as she recognized the man striding up the steps toward the street. Instinctively she reached down to switch off the stateroom light so she was in protective darkness as she saw Joe Miller walk purposefully to the car with the waiting chauffeur. Even as she watched, Joe slid into the front seat beside him.

She strained to see the driver's reaction, but the streetlight was too dim. All she could do was stay on the couch, hoping to see what else would happen.

A knock on her stateroom door at that moment made her swear softly. For an instant she debated ignoring it, but another, stronger one showed that her visitor wasn't going away. Probably the night stewardess, she thought irritably, and pulled the porthole curtains tightly closed before standing up and switching on the lamp again.

She reached the door just as the knocking resumed. "I'm coming—take it easy," she snapped, deciding that she'd get rid of her caller without delay so she could go back to her watching brief.

"Good God, don't you ever put on the chain?" Mitch countered when she yanked it open.

"Just come in and close the door," she snarled back. "Hurry up, will you?"

To Mitch's credit, he didn't stand there arguing. For once, he followed her instructions, and when she darted across to turn off the light again, he said, "This is a change. What's going on—or should I ask?"

"Don't be absurd," Miranda said, kneeling on the divan and twitching the drape aside. "I'm just being nosy, if you want the truth—oh, damn!"

"What's happened?" Mitch asked, stationing himself beside her. "It looks quiet out there."

"That's the trouble." Miranda flounced back against the cushion and turned on the light again. "The car's gone. The one that was parked up there complete with chauffeur when we came back from the nightclub."

A frown creased his forehead as he concentrated. "I remember. It was a more expensive model than most of the cars around here."

She nodded impatiently. "I even said something about it, but Joe didn't pay any attention. That's why I was surprised a few minutes ago when I saw him hightailing it up the steps for a tête-à-tête with the driver."

Mitch's eyebrows rose. "You're sure?"

"Of course I'm sure. And I'd bet next month's salary"—she cast him a wry sideways glance—"always supposing that I earn one . . ."

"Get on with it," he drawled.

"That apparently they were well-acquainted. Then you came knocking at the door—"

"—spoiling your surveillance," he finished for her. "I'm sorry."

She shrugged. "There was no way you could know. Besides, he probably had a perfectly reasonable explanation. Joe, I mean."

He nodded, but the frown was still in evidence. "Do you think he saw you?"

"I'm practically positive he didn't." She brushed her hair back absently. "That would be all I needed to cook my goose. As it was, he couldn't wait to get rid of me when we came back aboard. I thought it was because you were acting the heavy chaperon, but now I'm not so sure."

"You mean, he might have had another appointment?" Mitch looked thoughtful. "I'm inclined to think you're right." He reached up to make sure the drape was closed and made himself comfortable beside her. "There's no use giving him any more ideas if he comes back aboard."

"I have the feeling that seeing you would merely confirm his suspicions." When Mitch didn't show any signs of repentance, Miranda's tone became more severe. "If I'd had serious designs on the man, I'd really be annoyed with you. As it was . . ."

His eyebrows climbed. "Go on. Finish the sentence."

She shrugged. "He was simply a date—as you very well know. Even so, you needn't have been so hard on him." She didn't know whether to be annoyed or amused when Mitch yawned in the middle of her declaration. The latter won and she started to chuckle. "You look like the one who needs some sleep."

He stretched then, long legs barely fitting in the close quarters of the cabin. "I was tired before I went to check on Frieda tonight, and hospitals don't help your morale."

"I didn't realize you'd seen her. She *is* all right, isn't she?"

"She will be eventually. At the moment, she's suffering from concussion and they're keeping her quiet. I just dropped off some flowers and talked to the nurse in charge. She knew a little English, so we managed."

"Then Frieda doesn't know that her stateroom was ransacked?"

"I shouldn't think so. She won't get out of the hospital for a few days, but Gerhard says they'll cover for her on the rest of this trip. There's a chance she'll be on the next cruise, so she won't lose her job, after all." He got slowly to his feet. "Speaking of losing jobs, I'd better follow my own advice and let you get some sleep. Otherwise, neither one of us will be worth a damn in Szentendre tomorrow."

He almost sounded reluctant to leave, Miranda thought incredulously. Not only that, he was behaving nicely; almost as if he'd become reconciled to her writing the article. She swallowed and tried not to let the brief euphoria go to her head. Just because Mitch was acting in a civilized manner didn't mean that he was contemplating adding her name to the masthead of the magazine permanently. Probably his exemplary behavior was the closest she'd get to an apology for that kiss earlier in the day.

As he strolled toward the stateroom door, she could see that there wasn't any chance of him repeating his action, and she felt a pang of annoyance. Then she discovered that he'd stopped by the bureau and was looking at her inquisitively. "I beg your pardon," she said meekly.

"I asked if you were going to drag this thing along tomorrow?" He gestured toward her shoulder bag.

"Probably. It has all my belongings in it. That's why I carried it tonight."

"Apparently it's a feast or a famine with you."

"What do you mean by that?"

His gaze went over her slowly—starting at the rapidly beating pulse in her throat and moving down to linger deliberately on the soft curves of her breast. Miranda sensed that he'd disposed of her nylon robe and gown in his mind's eye—leaving her exposed to his masculine scrutiny and knowing she couldn't do a thing about it.

She reached up to pull her robe tighter and then felt anger surge through her as he grinned in response. "You didn't answer my question," she said, trying to match his *savoir faire* and not succeeding.

He apparently decided to stop baiting her and waved a careless hand toward her purse. "You will admit that it's a little on the bulbous side. I noticed it tonight when you were walking back to the ship. Tomorrow you'll need all your energy hiking up and down the hills of Szentendre."

"There are some things I can't do without," she said thoughtfully, opening the catch of the purse to peer inside. "I might need this tape recorder as well as—" She stopped in mid-sentence. "Good Lord, I'd forgotten all about it."

"What? The remains of your lunch?" Mitch asked, moving to look over her shoulder.

"Hardly. That was yesterday. No, seriously . . ." She dragged out the bud vase to show him. "It's my shopping triumph from this afternoon. Such a bargain that I'd forgotten that I was still carrying it around with me. It's not much," she explained as she saw him frown. "Frieda mentioned that they usually only have seconds in a shop like that one across the street."

"I didn't know that she collected china too." Mitch reached over and took it from her, checking the mark on the bottom.

"I don't think she does. As far as I know, she just bought the other one like this to take home as a present."

"This afternoon?" Mitch's voice was casual.

"That's right. When I bought mine." Miranda looked puzzled. "Why? Does it matter?"

"Probably not. We certainly can't ask her about it at the moment." He hoisted the vase appraisingly. "I'm not an expert, but I wouldn't think this was worth much more than fifteen dollars. Tell you what—why don't I ask Gerhard? There's not much that he doesn't know after being on this run so long."

"It seems sort of silly. A purser must have more important things on his mind."

"Keeping the passengers happy is top of his list," Mitch responded, and moved to open the stateroom door. "I'll give it back to you in the morning if that's okay. Now what's wrong?" he asked, noting her perplexed expression.

"You're being awfully nice all of a sudden."

"You mean I'm out of character?"

Her smile was apologetic. "Something of the sort."

"Don't worry—it won't last," he informed her, his voice taking on its accustomed assurance. "Now, for God's sake—go to bed. No more staring out windows. Besides, I wouldn't count on Joe's return. After striking out on his date with you, he's probably gone on to—"

"—better things?" After a moment's consideration, she added, "I guess you're right. I seem to be looking for bogeymen behind every bush since Durnstein."

"That comes from too much imagination and too little sleep." He stepped out into the hall and then spoiled his reassuring declaration by adding, "I'll wait here until you lock this door and put on the chain. And you are *not*, I repeat, *not*, to do any more socializing tonight."

Miranda stared back at him, wondering how she could ever have thought that his mood had softened.

"Did you hear what I said?"

She shrugged in defeat. "It means calling off the orgy, but I'll go along with it. This time."

Something flickered in his eyes, but it was gone so fast that she decided she must have imagined it. "I'm waiting," he said, staying where he was. "The door," he explained patiently.

Miranda gave him an exasperated glance and slammed it shut. Then she reached up and put the chain in place.

"Keep it that way," came Mitch's muttered comment from the other side.

After he had gone, Miranda remained leaning against the wooden door for a moment. If she had any intestinal fortitude, she would have been still seething over his high-handed manner. The fact that she wasn't—that she felt a definite twinge in her midsection—showed she must be cracking up. She frowned as she considered it, and then shook her head. Far more likely that the twinge came from hunger pangs after her sketchy dinner, she told herself, and walked over to turn down the divan bed.

A few minutes later, there was still a smile on her face when she fell soundly asleep.

8

Morning came much faster than usual.

When Miranda heard a knock on her stateroom and opened her eyes to see daylight rimming the porthole drape, she winced and pushed upright. "Who is it?" she called when the knock was repeated.

"Your breakfast, Miss Carey." Before Miranda could question such service, the male voice went on, "I'll leave it in the corridor for you. Mr. Emerson sent a message, too. *G' Morgen.*"

Miranda swung her legs to the floor and, still only half-awake, managed to reach the door. She started to release the chain and then remembered Mitch's warning from the night before. Unlocking the bolt, she pulled the door ajar and peered cautiously out into the corridor. The only thing that met her gaze was a breakfast tray resting just where the waiter had promised. She didn't waste any more time, unfastening the chain and bringing the tray inside. She used her hip to make sure the door was properly latched and then carried her breakfast over to the bureau.

She debated pouring a cup of coffee before reading the note on the tray, but decided against it. Her fingers shook as she opened the envelope, and then she sat down on the edge of her bed as the contents sank in. "Miranda," it started out in a forceful masculine hand. Apparently "Dear Miranda" wasn't in Mitch's scheme of things, she thought as her glance scanned the rest of the note. "Sorry—there's been a change of plans," it went on tersely. "I hope to meet you at Szentendre when your tour arrives. The major and his wife will look after you. Stay with them and *don't*"—the last word was underscored heavily and repeated—"*don't* miss the bus!"

Oh, great! Miranda thought, her lips tightening in annoyance. Not only had he deserted her—he'd appointed a couple of chaperons to make sure that she managed to find the tour group.

At least he'd remembered that she needed to eat breakfast, she thought as she poured coffee and surveyed a dish of grapefruit segments in juice. More juice than grapefruit, she decided, reaching for a spoon. She munched on a hard roll with cheese afterward and tried to pretend that it was preferable to scrambled eggs and bacon. At least she could eat it in comfort and not bother making conversation with the other passengers.

She left the tray atop the dressing table when she'd finished. A glance at her watch made her realize that she didn't have any time to waste if she caught the tour bus. As she headed for the shower, she flirted momentarily with the idea of ignoring the tour altogether and hiring other transportation to Szentendre—just to show Mitch that she wasn't helpless on her own. Then reason prevailed as she thought of how much a car rental would cost. Her nonexistent Hungarian was another factor as she visualized trying to ask directions along the way. The final clincher came ten minutes later when she was toweling herself dry after her shower. There was a knock on her stateroom door and then Janice Short's raised voice from the corridor.

"Miranda? It's Janice. Farrell and I will be waiting for you at the end of the gangway as soon as you're ready. Okay?"

"You don't have to bother," Miranda said, trying to fasten the towel around her as she opened the door a crack.

The major's wife was already on her way down the corridor, but she paused to smile over her shoulder. "It's no bother. And we promised Mitch. We wouldn't dare show up at Szentendre without you—he'd have our heads." She cast a quick glance at Miranda's towel, adding, "Better hurry—otherwise we'll be stuck at the back of the bus."

In a place where air conditioning was merely a wishful thought, it was a strong argument. Early on, Miranda had learned which vehicles were the Hungarian ones—they were without air conditioning or any other amenities. The tourist guides were bitter in their denunciations of the fact. One had even gone on to add that the most popular car on the streets of Budapest was made in East Germany. "We call them the 'plastic Mercedes,' " she'd said sarcastically, "and their most attractive feature is that nobody in his right mind would bother to steal one."

So the moral of the story was hurry to the bus, Miranda concluded. She reached for a cotton dress of apricot and white stripes which boasted a tucked front and full skirt. It fitted nicely and she added a pair of low-heeled pumps to accommodate Szentendre's hills and cobbled streets. Makeup was limited to a light application of lipstick and a dusting of powder, since she'd learned that the humidity made anything heavier a disaster. She did take time to splash on a refreshing citrus cologne before snatching up her purse and camera. A moment later, she let herself out of the stateroom and locked the door behind her.

There was a hurried exchange of "*Guten Morgens*," with the two crew members behind the purser's counter, but Gerhard wasn't in evidence so early in the day. Probably he was pulling rank, Miranda decided as she arrived at the end of the gangway.

Farrell and Janice Short were waiting ashore and Miranda couldn't miss seeing the relief on their faces as she appeared. Mitch must have used some powerful persuasion, she thought as she smiled in response. Normally, they wouldn't have been that ecstatic to share their day with an unattached female.

"I hope I didn't keep you waiting," Miranda began, only to have Janice catch her elbow and urge her to the steps and the waiting bus at the curbside.

"If we hurry, we can still get decent seats," Janice said. "Farrell, you go on ahead and try to hang on to some." Her husband, in seersucker trousers and a short-sleeved shirt, gave an understanding nod and sprinted away. "I'm not usually so demanding," Janice continued at Miranda's side, "but with this heat and no air conditioning, I have been known to get carsick." As Miranda's eyes widened, Janice giggled. "If I announce it when I get on a bus, there's usually no trouble at all getting a front seat. But if we're early enough—and I think we are," Janice continued, "I won't have to do anything drastic."

"You should have gone ahead," Miranda said as they started up the second set of steps to the curbside. "I would have found you on the bus."

"Mitch laid down the law . . ." Janice began, and then seemed to think better of it, finishing with a weak, "besides, it's nicer if we can sit together. Lord, it feels as if it's going to be a scorcher today. This is the coolest outfit I own and it's sticking to me already."

Miranda nodded sympathetically as her gaze ran quickly over Janice's striped short-sleeved top in yellow and blue with a slim blue cotton skirt. The only thing out of keeping was a bulging blue leather shoulder bag.

Janice saw her eyeing it and nodded grimly. "I don't know why I don't drop it overboard and carry my traveler's checks and visa in my teeth. I asked Farrell to carry just a couple of things at the beginning of the trip and he laughed at me." She shot a resigned glance in her husband's direction. "That's what comes from marrying a macho military type."

"Well, right now—I envy him his crew cut most of all," Miranda said to keep things light. "It's certainly the right kind of hairdo for a Hungarian heat wave."

Farrell Short was lounging across two seats behind the driver's and he beckoned them up the steps of the well-worn tour bus with a decisive gesture. "I can't hold on to these places much longer," he told his wife in a low tone. "For God's sake, sit down."

"Where's Miranda supposed to sit?" she asked, lingering in the aisle beside him.

"I put my camera case on the one behind us," he told them, standing up to retrieve it.

"Thanks very much," Miranda said, sliding into the window seat and trying to ignore some annoyed looks from passengers who had taken seats further to the rear. "I hope that we don't get knifed once we reach Szentendre," she said, keeping her voice down and leaning forward so that only the Shorts would hear. "If looks could kill, we've already been tried and sentenced."

"It's this damned humidity," Farrell Short said,

half-turning in his seat to talk to her. He pulled a handkerchief out and mopped his neck. "Want me to open your window further?"

Miranda reached up and pushed aside a dusty curtain which apparently served as a sunshade. "The catch is broken so the window has already gone as far as it can go. It doesn't matter—I'll be fine."

"At least this isn't a long trip," Janice put in. She waved a brochure from the ship. "If the bus goes there directly, it's only a short way upriver."

"Have you ever known a tour to take the short route anywhere?" her husband countered. "We're not due back at the ship until the late lunch, so they have to fill the time somehow. We'll be driven by every nook and cranny that has any significance in Hungarian history on the way. Even if it means the newest supermarket."

"You're a cynic," his wife told him.

"Five cents to a dollar says that I'm also right."

Janice turned to give Miranda a resigned look. "I learned during the first six months we were married to stop taking sucker bets like that."

"Because she lost most of them," Farrell put in smugly. "Hey, here comes our courier. Do you suppose that means we start on time?"

It was an encouraging thought, but the passengers soon found that it wasn't going to happen. By the time the last member of the group clambered aboard, the tour was fifteen minutes past their scheduled departure time and the temperature inside the bus felt as if it had risen by twenty degrees.

Major Short managed to give Miranda a triumphant grin when the tour guide announced that they would go through the Castle district of Buda before joining the main road leading to Szentendre. "Told you so," he said to Janice and Miranda.

"I don't mind so long as they keep moving." Janice told him. "That way, there's a little bit of a breeze coming in the window."

"Enjoy it while you can," her husband replied. "It'll be hotter than you-know-what by the time we're tromping around the cobblestones in Szentendre. I don't know why I let you talk me into this in the first place."

"Because it's supposed to be *the* arts center of the country," she retorted, waving a guidebook. Turning to Miranda, she added, "Farrell would do his sight-seeing at the bar of every Hilton in Europe if I didn't lay down the law."

"Right now, I wish I'd held firm," he said, mopping his face again. "Mitch was the only smart one in the crowd."

His comment was all Miranda needed to break in, asking casually, "Where *is* my boss? His note just said something about a change of plans."

Farrell shrugged. "Damned if I know. He got in touch with Gerhard at the crack of dawn. They work all hours at the purser's office."

"Then you didn't speak to Mitch himself?" Miranda persisted.

"No. Gerhard passed the word on to us. He was pretty specific about a strict chaperonage with you," Farrell said, a grin creasing his face. "We wondered what you've been up to."

"*You* wondered—I didn't," Janice said, casting Miranda a speaking look. "And they talk about women being busybodies. Honestly!"

"If I could have your attention, please—" came the guide's voice as she paused in the aisle and directed a stern gaze at them. "I am sorry there is no public-address system, so there will have to be quiet. That way, everybody can hear."

Janice wilted under her directive and turned to face the front again. Miranda hid a smile and focused her attention out the window, aware of the courier's explanations, but really not listening. The same information was in her pamphlets and the guide's heavily accented English was difficult to understand.

The bus trip was pleasant and low-key when they finally wound their way out of the city limits of Budapest. Look-alike concrete apartment complexes with dirt landscaping gave way to softer and more agreeable views as they entered the countryside. Multiple-dwelling buildings were soon replaced by modest single-family homes mainly of stucco or brick topped with tile roofs. There were very few patches of lawn and most color was supplied by the carefully tended vegetable and flower gardens. The Hungarians could have vied with the Japanese for space utilization, Miranda thought, as healthy plants seemed to occupy every available inch of land. Occasionally the bus passed massive commercial greenhouses which were set back from the two-lane road. Their surroundings were enclosed by fences made with concrete posts, which gave the acreage a depressing atmosphere. Miranda decided the places resembled American correctional institutions and then concluded that her imagination was running rampant. Far better to enjoy the scenery with picturesque locust and horse-chestnut trees overhanging the roadway.

She found herself wondering what Mitch would have to say when she arrived in Szentendre, and glanced at the empty seat beside her. Was he going to occupy it on the way back to Budapest, or perhaps

he'd have other plans for the two of them! Miranda
drew a deep breath and reached for her booklet which
described the artists' colony—at least she could be
planning the best places to spend her time, in case he
asked about her proposed schedule for the outing.

She was so engrossed in her thoughts that she
looked up in surprise a little later when the guide
announced they were arriving at their destination.
The Danube was winding along the road on their
right-hand side and a quick look to the left showed a
vista of old church spires amidst eighteenth-century
buildings on the hillside.

"You will remember that this charming town had
its beginnings in the second century with the Romans," the guide was saying. "However, there are
remnants of history from the 1600's, when refugees
who were escaping Turkish invaders settled here.
Kindly do not leave any item of value on the bus,"
the guide went on, getting back to the commonplace,
"as the driver will not be here all the time. You must
be back at the scheduled time, so that you will arrive
back at your ship for the late luncheon serving. If
you are not on time, we do not wait."

"So much for us," Janice said, getting up when the
bus driver pulled to an empty space along the curb.
"We'd better not cut it too fine."

"If you would like to go with me, please line up on
the curb," the guide ordered as she signaled for the
driver to open the door. "Those of you who want to
be on your own, please remember the name of this
street. The more interesting parts of the town are up
on the hillside near the main square.

Farrell Short gestured Miranda into the aisle ahead
of him, so that she could follow Janice, and heaved
a breath of relief once they got down on the curbside.

"Fresh air," he said happily. "And fresher than it was in Budapest, or I miss my guess."

"That's because we're out of that smog," Janice said, looking around. "I could do without the cobblestones, though. "They'll be murder to walk on."

"They provide atmosphere—that's what you're paying for. Don't you agree, Miranda?" Farrell asked.

She turned back, frowning. "I beg your pardon?"

"It doesn't matter. What's bothering you?"

"I don't see Mitch." Her gaze searched the sidewalk and throngs around them. "Did he ever say where he'd meet us?"

Farrell tried to concentrate. "Not exactly. But he must be around someplace. There's no point in waiting here, though."

Janice pulled out her handkerchief to dab at her forehead. "Maybe it's cooler at the top of the hill. C'mon, Miranda—let Mitch catch up with you."

"My feelings exactly," Miranda agreed, determined not to show her disappointment. "There are too many things to see to waste time hanging around here. How about taking in the square and then that gallery of Margit Kovacs' collection?"

"Sounds good," Janice said, starting toward the narrow winding street leading up the hillside. "Kovacs' ceramic art has an international reputation and I'm dying to see it."

"I'd feel more like absorbing culture if we absorbed something cool to drink first," Farrell told his wife. "Let's investigate the taverns around the square."

"No way. This time we act like tourists first," she announced, "then you can behave naturally. *If* I don't break an ankle on these cobblestones."

"You would wear those shoes . . ." he reminded her. "I told you they were a mistake."

Miranda tuned out their domestic wrangling as she climbed up the narrow street. She was trying not to miss any of the sights; the gabled houses on the far side of the block where stone stairways provided the only access—the stamp-size gardens and window boxes providing charming patches of color against gray and yellowed stone walls.

There were innumerable covered patios with patrons already occupying the tables. Most were drinking beer and wine, but there were a few studying the menus, which were on chalkboards next to the kitchen. From the appetizing smells coming from those quarters, Miranda felt a momentary regret that they were going back to the ship to eat.

Farrell apparently shared her feelings. "Gosh, smell those onions," he enthused as they passed a popular tavern where they could stare into an open kitchen. "That must be goulash of some kind he's whipping up. Look at those green peppers and—"

"C'mon." Janice pulled at his elbow. "Keep going or you'll gain five pounds just looking."

"But that was a cold tomato soup they were serving, with fresh mushrooms floating on top—"

"Darling—it's too early for lunch. Even for a snack. I promise we can come back. If we stop off here now, I'll never get to see that Kovacs collection."

"Okay, sweetie." He patted her hand and kept on walking. "First things first. I just wonder where in the devil that gallery is."

Miranda was consulting her guidebook. "It says here that it's at *One Vastagh Gyorgy utca*—wherever that could be. I wish I knew some Hungarian."

Farrell pulled up as they reached the top of the street and found themselves in a picturesque town square thronged with visitors and townspeople. "Wait here," he instructed. "I see somebody over there who looks like a tour guide. I'll go ask. Incidentally, you might keep an eye out for Mitch," he added to Miranda.

"I will." She chewed uncertainly on the edge of her lower lip. "I didn't think there'd be so many people in this place."

"I know what you mean," Janice said after Farrell had hurried off in search of directions. "This is going to be a crowd scene instead of the sleepy little town in the countryside that I thought it would be." She fanned herself with a guidebook to create a breeze. "My Lord, it's hot! I don't know how you manage to look so cool," she added, giving Miranda a querulous look.

"It's strictly an optical illusion. I'm beginning to see why all those people were sitting around in that shaded patio."

"I know. Oh, look! Farrell's motioning to us." Janice pointed across the square. "He must have gotten directions to the gallery."

They hurried across to join him and he pointed down a narrow alleyway between two old stone buildings. "One block down this way—at least that's what one guide said. If I understood his French."

"But you only had two years of French in high school," Janice reminded him as she fell into step.

He shrugged. "If it isn't in the next block, I'll find a German-speaking guide. I had three years of that," he announced to Miranda with a grin.

At the end of the block, they discovered there was no need to look further, as the throngs of people going through an archway on the left identified the Kovacs gallery.

"Stay here," Farrell said, urging them into a niche

just inside the entrance. "I'll stand in line to buy the tickets."

"Let me give you some money," Miranda said, starting to root in her purse.

"You can buy me a drink later," he said, waving her suggestion aside as he hurried to the end of the ticket queue.

"Gosh, do you suppose it's as mobbed inside?" Janice wondered aloud as she and Miranda moved back against the wall to be out of the way.

"I hope not. If it is, we'll be lucky to even get a glance at the exhibits. Everybody must have read the same guidebook," she added disconsolately.

"And Mitch will never find us in the mob. Oh, well—his loss is our gain. We can keep each other company sightseeing later on, because if I know my husband, he's going to fall by the wayside."

"Who's taking my name in vain?" Farrell asked, reappearing at their side.

"Never mind. That didn't take long," Janice replied in surprise.

"It isn't difficult to spend money," he assured her, handing a ticket to each of them. "Now, follow me—we might as well elbow our way into the horde. That's the only way we'll get in the place."

It was a crush, they discovered, but after the first five minutes they agreed it was worth the effort. The examples of Hungary's famed exponent of ceramic art were breathtaking in their simplicity and beauty. The displays had been carefully contrived and viewers were treated to subterranean corridors as well as long sunlit areas where they could linger to appreciate the finer details of the ceramic pieces. Miranda and Janice were especially taken with a realistic grouping of fishermen's wives, each face reflecting uncertainty and anxiety as the women waited on shore for their returning husbands. "Even the hands are sculptured to reveal their despair," Miranda commented, turning to Janice. And then, observing her more closely, said, "Good Lord, you look as unhappy as they do. What's the matter?"

"It's this heat," Janice said, putting her palms to her white cheeks. "I don't think I can take it any longer. Is Farrell . . . ?"

"I'm here, love," her husband said, appearing suddenly at her side. "What's the matter?"

"Junior's making waves," she replied with a tremulous smile. "I think I'd better go somewhere and sit down."

"Right away." He caught her in a firm grasp around the waist. "We'll go back to the square and find a table in the shade. Miranda, you stay here and finish your sightseeing. You can find us there afterward."

"Are you sure? Isn't there anything I can do?"

"I'll be fine as soon as I can rest where it's cool. And so will Junior," Janice told Farrell. "Take that worried look off your face—I'm not about to let anything happen to the unborn generation."

"My wife—the liberated woman," he said, dropping a quick kiss on her cheek. "Look for us in the square, Miranda."

Miranda nodded and watched Farrell whisk his wife through the crowded gallery and down some steps out of sight. That bit of news meant she'd have to look around for a baby present and give it to Janice before the end of the cruise. It was a pity that the Kovacs gallery didn't sell reproductions, because there was a charming Madonna figure with an infant at her breast which would have made a wonderful gift. Wandering into the next corridor, she caught sight of another familiar figure leaning against a pillar. She hurried through a group of people admiring a geometric sculpture to Elsa Miller's side, saying, "I thought I recognized you. Are you all right? Lean against me—"

"Oh, Miranda" There was indescribable relief in the older woman's voice. "Thank heaven you're here. Does it seem stifling in this place to you?"

"Absolutely boiling. Having all these people around doesn't help. Janice Short felt the same way and had to give up a few minutes ago."

"That helps soothe my ego." Elsa fanned her flushed features with a lacy handkerchief. "I thought it was just because I'm so ancient. Joe warned me not to try to do too much."

"Is he around?" Miranda was trying to see beyond the clumps of people at the far end of the gallery.

"No. I told him it wasn't necessary to ride herd on me here. He's seen all this before and I didn't want to impose on him today." Elsa drew a shaky breath and then pulled herself erect with an effort. "I'll be fine if I can get out in the fresh air again."

Miranda put an arm around her shoulders and guided her toward the exit. "I hope this is the right way—"

"You just have to take me to the door—I don't want to interrupt your sightseeing."

Elsa did her best to sound firm, but Miranda heard a quiver that indicated she wasn't happy about the situation. "Don't be absurd," Miranda reassured her, "I'm glad of an excuse to escape the crowds too. Maybe we can find that restaurant in the square and join forces with Farrell and Janice."

"That's kind of you to suggest it, my dear—"

"It sounds like fun," Miranda assured her, surprised to find how her own interest in sightseeing had dwindled since Mitch hadn't kept his end of the bargain. "After all, we can read the guidebook and see what we've missed when we get back on the ship."

"Getting back to the ship sounds like the best thing that could happen," Elsa said, her voice more tremulous than usual. "Thank heaven for your sense of direction—this is the entrance ahead of us, isn't it?"

"Absolutely. Let's stay over to the right and avoid the mobs coming in." Miranda was steering her gently ahead of her as she spoke. "We should come out on the street. Although this cobblestone lane looks more like an alley than anything else," she concluded when they'd gotten through the gate and passed two French tour groups lining up to enter the gallery. "I wonder which is the shortest way to the square?"

"My dear, if you wouldn't mind—I think I'd better head back to the ship," Elsa said, putting a detaining hand on her arm.

"But I don't think the buses will leave for quite a while—"

"Thank heaven, that doesn't matter to me. I came by car and my driver should be waiting. He's parked down by the river."

"Then I'll walk you back and make sure you get safely on your way," Miranda assured her, keeping a firm grip on Elsa's elbow as they started down the lane. "I have scads of time before the tour gathers."

"If you'd like to leave earlier, you'd be most welcome to come with me," Elsa offered politely. "It's the least I can do after you've been so kind."

"Actually, I think I'd better go back and find Farrell and Janice. I did promise I'd meet them later," Miranda said.

"Of course. I understand." Elsa glanced around them. "At least, we know we're going the right way. The river's at the bottom and the town is at the top."

"That's fortunate, because a good sense of direction isn't one of my shining qualities." Miranda was tempted to linger as they passed an attractive shop window, but resisted after a quick sideways glance at Elsa's pale cheeks. Obviously the heat was still bothering her, so she was probably wise to hurry back to the air-conditioned comforts of the ship. "I'm surprised there aren't more people wandering around down here," Miranda said, trying for a safe topic to keep Elsa's mind off the weather. "The streets were so crowded up by the square."

"Because of the tourists, my dear." Elsa's voice had a cynical ring. "Haven't you noticed—it doesn't matter which side of the Iron Curtain you're on. The ring of the cash register is always the most important thing." She frowned slightly as a thought occurred to her. "Why isn't Mitch with you? I thought he was interested in making sure that you could write about Szentendre properly."

Miranda tried for a diplomatic answer as they reached the bottom of the hill. "Actually, he was supposed to meet me earlier, but something must have gone wrong. Is your driver parked along here?"

"Just down the block—that dark blue sedan at the curb," Elsa said, gesturing feebly. "I can manage if you want to rejoin your friends."

"Of course not. I'll see you inside and safely on your way." Miranda allowed herself a small grin as they trudged on down the sidewalk which bordered the river. Elsa hadn't relinquished her grip one iota. She clearly wanted a companion along despite her assurances to the contrary.

It was just as they reached the sedan where a uniformed driver was getting out of the car that Elsa drew up in surprise. "My dear Miranda, you'd better—no, that's silly. He probably has a perfectly logical explanation."

Miranda's brows drew together. "I don't know what you're talking about."

"Not what—whom," Elsa snapped back irritably. "He's over there across the street. You'd better get behind Stefan if you don't want them to see you."

Miranda instinctively moved behind the chauffeur even as she protested, "What do you mean—them?"

"Mitch and that tall brunette. She must have driven him here, since she's locking that car. Attractive, too, and with good clothes sense. Black and white is such a satisfactory color combination in the summer, don't you think, Miranda?" She glanced up for confirmation and then asked anxiously, "What is it, dear? You don't look at all well."

Miranda shook her head, trying to disprove her accusation. "I'm fine. Just fine," she managed after taking a deep breath. She was dimly aware that circumstances had changed; Elsa had indicated to the chauffeur that she didn't need assistance, but that her guest did, and Miranda felt a strong masculine hand under her arm for support. Ordinarily she would have shaken it off, but somehow that glance of Mitch sharing a laughing moment with his beautiful companion had dealt her the equivalent of a blow to the solar plexus. Like a wounded animal, she tried to push behind the chauffeur, so that Mitch wouldn't catch a glimpse of her stricken state.

Elsa sensed her unhappiness, hesitating before she stepped into the back seat. "Are you sure that you don't want to go back to Budapest with me? Stefan

can give Mitch a message for you—if you'd rather
not deliver it in person. They're still looking in shop
windows, so it wouldn't be difficult," she added,
aware of Miranda's averted gaze. "But you'll have to
make up your mind, my dear, because they're starting this way. As a matter of fact, I think he's seen
you."

"Then let's just go," Miranda said as she bolted
into the car beside her.

Elsa nodded understandingly, saying something in
German to the driver which made him slam the door.
An instant later, he'd slid behind the wheel and they
were pulling away from the curb.

"Miranda! What in the hell do you think you're
doing?" Mitch's angry shout came distinctly to her
ears and it wasn't until they were halfway down the
block that she risked a glimpse through the back
window.

He was still on the curb staring after her, and it
didn't take the brunette's startled expression or the
faces of the passersby to know that he was turning
the air blue at the unexpected turn of events.

Elsa peered through the window too, and her expression was rueful when she shifted in the seat to
face the front again. "I hope," she said tactfully, "you
weren't planning on a long career working for the
man."

Miranda managed a thin smile. "At this rate, I'll be
lucky if he lets me stay aboard ship for the rest of the
cruise. Probably I shouldn't have ducked out like
that, but suddenly—"

Elsa reached over to pat her hand when her voice
broke. "I know, my dear. Life is never easy, but
somehow one never realizes how dreadful it can become. It's like a bad dream, only the real horror

comes when you find it's broad daylight and there's no escape. For any of us."

Miranda stayed silent as she saw Elsa stare fixedly out the car window on her side. A glance toward the front showed the chauffeur's broad shoulders as he drove swiftly back toward Budapest. She closed her eyes, resisting an impulse to rest her head against the glass of the window beside her, able only to think how wonderful it would be to reach her stateroom on the ship. Then she could lock out the world and howl into her pillow like all the other misguided women whose hearts had ruled their heads—only to suffer the consequences.

9

It seemed to take forever for them to arrive back at the ship. As they approached the inner-city districts of Budapest, the traffic was heavy despite the stifling heat, which made pedestrians seek any available shade. Dust hung in the heavy air and a cleaner wielding a crude broom on the sidewalk was literally sweeping up a storm. Miranda started to mention it to Elsa, but seeing her withdrawn expression, decided against it.

She was surprised that the chauffeur didn't offer his services when they finally pulled up at the curb closest to the quay. After opening the door for them a moment later, he appeared rooted at the curb. Miranda had planned a hasty exit, but good manners forced her to offer Elsa a helping hand down the steps to the pier and finally onto the gangway. And naturally when she would have welcomed the sight of some crew members—the entire deck was deserted. Apparently the crew of the *Donau* was taking every advantage of shore time.

She felt Elsa sway slightly at her side and turned to her anxiously. "You really should have a stewardess or someone to look after you. I don't suppose Joe is aboard."

Any hope of reassurance disappeared as Elsa shook

her head. "Probably I'll feel much better once I lie down," she said in quavery tones. "If you could just take me down the corridor—"

"Nonsense," Miranda cut in, "you'll come to my stateroom and rest. At least until I can find someone who can look after you in your quarters. Just hang on to me," she added, urging Elsa along the empty hallway. "My key should be in my purse somewhere—here it is! At the bottom, naturally." She kept up a cheerful monologue until they reached her door. "Thank heaven for the air conditioning. You'll feel better after you lie down for a few minutes in here where it's cool. Take the divan under the porthole and I'll give you this extra pillow." She saw Elsa seated and moved to get the pillow she'd mentioned, only to stare saucer-eyed when she turned back. She found a far different older woman sitting upright on the divan and pointing a pistol at her with a steady hand. "My God! What are you doing with that thing?"

"Sit down on the bed, Miranda, and don't try anything foolish," Elsa said, waving the gun to emphasize her words. The quavery undertone in her voice had vanished and there was a determined look on her face that made Miranda obey her command instinctively. "Pay attention, because there isn't much time," Elsa continued with a glance at the diamond-studded watch on her wrist. "Without making any silly moves, I want you to give me that vase you bought yesterday. If you follow directions," she added, "you won't suffer. On the other hand, if you try anything clever, I won't hesitate to use this gun. I assure you it won't be the first time, and I have too much at stake to even hesitate. Now—get the vase!"

The situation was so bizarre that Miranda was physically unable to stir. Then, seeing Elsa's expression harden, she said hastily, "It isn't here. Honestly, that's the truth. Mitch took it last night." The last sentence came out as Elsa brought the gun up from her lap. "If you mean the bud vase from that funny little shop on the corner—"

"Why did he want it?" Elsa's questions cut into Miranda's sentence like a honed knife.

Miranda tried to think. "I'm . . . I'm not sure. He said something about checking the value of it with Gerhard. The purser."

"I *know* who Gerhard is"—Elsa's features bore a look of distaste— "and I don't think much of your story. Mitch would know that there wasn't any value to a vase like that."

"But then why . . . ?" Miranda's voice trailed off again when she realized that Elsa would hardly furnish any information under the circumstances.

"Why am I so anxious to get it?" the older woman finished the sentence for her. She rose from the divan, gesturing resolutely with the gun. "My dear Miranda, you are in no position to ask questions. Empty those drawers," she commanded, pointing toward the dressing table. "I want to see for myself that you're telling the truth."

Miranda moved quickly to obey, aware by then that Elsa was in deadly earnest. The older woman stayed out of reach so that any hope of disarming her wasn't practical. There wasn't even anything handy to throw in her direction, Miranda thought in some disgust as she rummaged through her belongings. Certainly the pitcher of ice water atop the dresser was too heavy for quick maneuvering, and the pamphlets next to it were utterly useless.

She looked up inquiringly when she'd finally emptied the bottom drawer, and saw Elsa point toward the closet. "Clear that top shelf and then open your suitcases."

"They're under the bed," Miranda told her.

"Then I suggest you move them in a hurry," Elsa snapped.

"Honestly, it isn't here," Miranda said, after taking a pair of shoes from the top shelf of her closet, leaving it empty. "If it's so important for you to have one of the darned things—why don't you ask Frieda? She bought a vase at the same time."

"So we discovered," Elsa replied. "The suitcases, girl. I want to see inside them."

So Frieda's vase wasn't the one they wanted. Miranda was thinking as she knelt to pull her luggage from under the bed. But why? It was an exact duplicate, or appeared to be. She shook her head to clear it and unzipped her luggage as Elsa watched from the far end of the stateroom.

The older woman's breathing could be heard plainly in the quiet of the cabin as Miranda mutely displayed her empty cases and then shoved them back under the bed again. "I wish you'd believe me," she said, straightening. "I don't know why Mitch took the vase—if you want to wait until he comes back to the ship, we can ask him first thing."

Elsa's sharp laugh didn't have a vestige of humor in it. "You're just fool enough to think that might work. It's too bad you got yourself involved in this, Miranda—I don't know whether it was deliberate or just bad luck, but unfortunately there's no pulling out now." She stood up in sudden decision. "Come— we'll go back to the car. Stefan has been waiting just in case of an emergency."

"But where are we going?" Miranda asked, trying to ignore the gun held ready in Elsa's hand.

"I haven't decided yet."

"Well, I'm not going," Miranda announced, deciding to make a stand. "You wouldn't dare use that gun aboard ship. Half of the crew would keep you from even reaching the gangway. If you're smart, you'll put it away and I'll try to forget that you—"

"You ignorant fool!" Elsa had never looked more formidable as she interrupted ruthlessly. "I'd use it in a minute. At this point, I have nothing to lose. Why do you think we're aboard this . . . this scow in the first place?"

Miranda looked around the cabin, uncomprehending. Aside from the clutter of her belongings, there was certainly nothing wrong with the room. "I wouldn't exactly call this the ghetto," she said finally.

"What would you know about it?" Elsa made a decisive gesture. "Unlock that door and stay close when we get out in the corridor. I'll have the gun on you every minute."

Miranda's thoughts raced as she took a step toward the door. Any kind of escape attempt would have to be before they left the ship. The little time she'd spent with Stefan, the chauffeur, had convinced her that the man was an automaton who followed Elsa's orders without question. If she decreed that they should start out with a passenger and return alone, he wouldn't turn a hair.

"I said—move!" Elsa commanded from behind her, giving Miranda a painful jab in the back with the muzzle of the gun. "Open that door carefully and then step aside. I want to make sure that the corridor is deserted. Don't try anything foolish," she ordered when Miranda hesitated after unlocking the door.

Miranda moved reluctantly out of Elsa's way, her mind racing as she considered the possibilities. There'd be an instant when Elsa's attention was on the corridor—it had to be the best time to try to get the gun away from her. If only she could move fast enough!

Miranda edged imperceptibly closer as Elsa pulled the door open a fraction more. She waited until her gray head poked cautiously around the frame and then launched herself onto Elsa's back, grappling desperately to hold on to her gun hand.

Her attack sent them sprawling on the corridor rug, Elsa emitting an outraged screech on the way down. She didn't let go of the gun, though, and Miranda struggled to stay on top of her and get control of it. Despite her age, the older woman flailed in a frenzy to free herself. Miranda saw her finger start to tighten on the trigger and lurched across her in a final frantic attempt to knock the pistol out of reach.

At the same moment, Elsa slithered out from under and managed to get to her knees. The force of her movement shunted Miranda headfirst toward the corridor wall. There was only a split second to realize what was happening before she collided with the wood and whimpered in pain.

She moaned again when hard hands pulled her upright and deposited her on the carpeted hallway with such force that her senses reeled. "That hurts," she protested.

"Stop complaining. I ought to break your neck," snarled a familiar masculine voice in her ear.

Miranda had recovered enough to recognize Mitch's tall figure as he bent over her. "I think you already have," she managed to flare back, determined that she wouldn't let him know how glad she was to see him. "You didn't have to toss me around like a sack of potatoes."

"If I had my way, you wouldn't be able to sit on the carpet even now. Only the fact that I was taught never to hit a woman saved a few other choice bits of your anatomy." He moved aside just enough that two uniformed men holding on to a subdued Elsa could get past them in the corridor.

Miranda opened her mouth to ask what was going on, when she saw the brunette that Mitch had been with at Szentendre, in earnest conversation with Gerhard and another uniformed man at the stairway.

"Hungarian police," Mitch put in, reading Miranda's mind with his usual competence.

"The brunette?"

"Hardly. She's an acquaintance from our embassy, who's helping round up the gang. Joe's incarcerated in the lounge, talking so fast that we should have all the information we want in practically no time."

Miranda chose to ignore his smug tone. "What about Stefan?"

"What about him? I mean, who the hell's Stefan?"

"You have all the answers," Miranda replied, glowering up at him. "I'm surprised that you don't know that one. And let go of my elbow—you're cutting off the circulation."

Mitch loosened his grip, but pursued his main interest with terrierlike determination. "I asked you a question—who's Stefan?"

Miranda struggled to her feet, surprised to find that her knees seemed unwilling to accept her weight.

She sagged against the wall and tried to look as if she'd planned it that way as she replied, "The driver who brought us back from Szentendre. Elsa said that the car was still waiting up at the curb—it's where we were headed when you crashed the party. That's why I jumped her and tried to get the gun. I got the idea that it was going to be a one-way trip for me." She rubbed her cheek wearily with the back of her hand. "After this, I won't tangle with any little old ladies. I must be out of shape, because she was on the way toward making mincemeat out of me when you came along."

"So I noticed. If I won't be accused of mauling you again, how about a helping hand so you can get into the stateroom? Before you fall flat on your face all by yourself," Mitch added, raking her with a critical gaze.

Miranda nodded reluctantly. "It would be nice to sit down for a few minutes."

Mitch uttered a smothered comment that didn't sound polite as he put an arm around her waist, steering her into her cabin nearby. He let out an amazed whistle as he saw her belongings strewn around the room.

"Elsa's idea," Miranda said before he could ask any questions. "She wanted to find that damned bud vase that you ran off with last night."

"You mean she put you through all this"—Mitch's gesture encompassed the ransacked stateroom—"because of that?"

"It was a good part of it." Miranda sank onto the edge of the nearest bed and gave him an angry look. "Of course, if you'd managed to keep your appointment to meet me in Szentendre, probably the whole thing would never have happened. Where *is* my vase, by the way?"

He ignored that, saying, "I'd better go tell that policeman and Marilyn about your friend Stefan. They'll want to ask him some questions."

"They're not the only one with some questions," Miranda pointed out in a tart voice as he reached for the doorknob. "When I finish my article, I'm going to demand a bonus for hazardous duty—like serving on the front lines."

He glanced casually over his shoulder. "You must be feeling better. With a little rest, you should be back to normal in no time. Although"—he paused with the door halfway open to look at her thoughtfully— "I'm not sure that I don't prefer you after you've lost a couple of falls in the corridor wrestling match."

"That's the nicest compliment I've had all day." She raised her voice when he took another step into the corridor. "When you come back, I'd like to have my vase."

The door was almost closed, but he poked his head around the jamb to say, "I gave it to Marilyn. I'll try to get it back eventually, if you feel strongly about it."

"The brunette?" Miranda's voice rose in anger. "You've a hell of a nerve giving her my vase."

His glance was just as annoyed as hers. "Calm down. I'll buy you a dozen of them, if they're so important. Get some rest and you'll feel better."

The door closed behind him with a bang.

Miranda glowered at it and then leaned back on the bed, wondering whether she'd gotten the headache which was pounding behind her temples from her struggle with Elsa or after he'd mentioned handing over her vase to the brunette.

One thing she *did* know for certain: she wasn't

following his orders any longer. She was not going to rest—that was definite. As soon as she relaxed a minute or so, she'd get up and find some aspirin.

That should take care of the headache.

After that, she'd sit down and write a letter of resignation, which should take care of everything else.

10

An interval of sobbing on her bed didn't improve her morale.

"Idiot!" she told herself a few minutes later as she reached for a handkerchief and blew her nose. Crying didn't solve anything—it just gave her a stuffed-up nose which made her headache worse. She got up to lock the stateroom door before taking off her clothes and starting for the shower. Hot water might do as much good as aspirin, she decided, and if it didn't help, she could always take the pills later.

There really wasn't time to be a hypochondriac, she was thinking as she stepped under the shower and held her face up to the welcome cascade of hot water. So her hair got soaked too—it really didn't matter. At that moment, all she wanted was to wash away any lingering remnants of the day's happenings.

She felt considerably refreshed afterward and toweled her hair briefly before slipping on the Turkish toweling robe hanging from a hook on the door. The aspirin could wait, she decided, and made a face at herself in the mirror.

Her reflection wasn't great; pink-rimmed eyelids were a legacy from the tears, and there wasn't an iota of color in her cheeks. She pulled her damp hair back and fastened it with a bandeau before dropping her towel on the rack. At least she was clean—and she wasn't apt to be entertaining visitors.

That thought sobered her for a moment until she gave herself a mental poke and went out to straighten up the stateroom. Even though her plans were uncertain about finishing the cruise, there wasn't any point in leaving reminders of Elsa's visit.

Once she'd put her clothes back on the hangers and straightened the dressing-table drawers, she took a piece of stationery from the pad given to passengers when they boarded. A picture of the *Donau* at the top of the paper brought a twinge of unhappiness as she stared at it, recalling the high hopes she'd had at the beginning of the voyage. Certainly she'd never anticipated falling head over heels in love with an employer who reacted to her presence like a man who ended up with a handful of nettles after he'd reached for buttercups.

She bit her lip as she tried to remember the proper form for a letter of resignation; wondering whether she should offer to reimburse Mitch for her transatlantic passage money as well. She thought of her current bank balance and then did some mental arithmetic. The result made her wince, but her chin firmed and she started writing. A graceful exit might come high, but it was important to achieve.

She was down to the third paragraph, struggling over whether to make her farewell final or whether to leave the door ajar, so to speak. Just in case Mitch might have second thoughts in the months to come. Her eyes grew dreamy at that fantasy, and the abrupt knock at the door made her jerk with surprise. She started to call "Come in" and then decided that she'd better fasten the chain lock before seeing who was in the corridor.

"I'm glad that you're finally using your head." Mitch's wry comment greeted her as she peered suspiciously around the jamb seconds later. "Hurry up and let me in before I get frostbite." He held up a bottle of champagne in one hand and two icy tulip glasses in the other.

Miranda opened her lips to protest his newest invasion, but subsided when he kicked the bottom of the door to reinforce his order. "Don't you ever say 'please' or 'thank you'?" she complained as she unfastened the chain and stepped back.

"Occasionally." He put the champagne down next to the pitcher of ice water and deposited the glasses at the other end of the tray. "Lock the door again." He glanced over his shoulder in time to see her lips thin in a rebellious line. "Please."

An instant later when the chain lock was back in place, his "Thank you" was delivered with appropriate solemnity.

Color flared momentarily in Miranda's cheeks, but she stuck to her guns. "You're welcome," she said, matching his tone. "Now—what was it you wanted to see me about?"

His mouth twitched as if he was having trouble containing his amusement, but he didn't let it show in his voice. "For one thing, I wanted to return this," he said, extracting her bud vase from the hip pocket of his gray flannel slacks.

Miranda frowned as she took it, embarrassed that she'd made such a fuss about it earlier. "You mean that your friend Marilyn didn't need it any longer?"

"Oh, this isn't the same one," he said easily, turned to peel the gold foil from the neck of the champagne bottle. "I asked Gerhard to find another one. This one was stored with the ship's supplies for that gift counter in the hairdressing salon. Apparently he picked up a dozen or so the last time they were in port."

"You mean he had Herend china on the ship all along?" Miranda wailed, remembering all the walking she'd done to find a piece. "Why on earth didn't Frieda mention it?"

"She didn't know. At least, that's what I'm guessing. Don't forget she had some time off before this voyage."

Miranda nodded, thinking about it. "That makes sense. Otherwise she wouldn't have bought one where I did." Her head jerked up when the cork flew off the champagne and she watched Mitch hastily pour the bubbling liquid into the two glasses he'd brought. When he held one out to her, her hand was slow in coming up. "If you've come to fire me," she said hesitantly, "you don't have to soften the blow with champagne."

"Oh, for God's sake!" He pushed the glass into her fingers so forcefully that some of the contents sloshed over the side. His frown smoothed as he saw her calmly mop up the overflow with the bottom of her terry robe. "At least it comes in handy for something," he growled. "Why don't you take your drink with you and put on some clothes? I'd hate to have you get any more wrong ideas."

Miranda didn't move. "You mean, I'm not going to be fired?"

A brief crooked grin erased his exasperated expression. "Let's say that you could convince me to change my mind about that. And you don't have to suspect the champagne. I just thought we needed a break, and there's a mob of people up in the lounge."

Miranda was still thinking about his first comment

as she replied absently to the second. "I wonder why. You'd think they'd all be ashore."

"In this weather, sightseeing takes a second place to air conditioning." He took a sip of his champagne and looked around, finally going over to settle on the other divan, stretching his feet out on the coffee table in front of him and heaving a sigh of relief. Only then did he bestow a quizzical look on her. "You're really amazing! No questions—after all you've gone through?"

"Just one," she said, burying her nose in the bubbles and taking another sip. "And you side stepped it."

He didn't rise to that, saying instead, "I gather that you didn't suffer any lasting ill effects from your roll on the carpet with Elsa?"

"Of course not. I still can't believe it happened," she added, staring pensively at the glass in her hand. "Maybe that's why I stayed so long in the shower—I wanted to wash away everything connected with the afternoon. Freud would have a few things to say about that, wouldn't he?"

"I think he'd say it was abnormal to retain any other kind of reaction," Mitch replied. His sympathetic tone hardened, however, as he went on, "I would like to know what in the hell you were doing with her in the first place. I ran into Farrell and Janice a few minutes ago and they were still upset that you didn't meet them at the square in Szentendre as planned."

"I intended to . . ." Miranda said, trying to think what she could use as a legitimate excuse. Certainly she wasn't going to admit that it was the brief view of his arrival—arm in arm with the beautiful Marilyn— that had prompted her flight.

"It's a damned good thing I caught a glimpse of you getting into the car with Elsa and decided to follow you," Mitch said in a stern voice. "If I'd been a little closer, I could have saved you the bother at this end."

Miranda recalled what she'd endured in the stateroom with Elsa's gun trained on her, and decided that "bother" was an understatement.

Her feelings must have been evident, because Mitch's eyes narrowed as he considered her across the room. "The old lady was unhinged, you know, and we underestimated her all along. If we'd had any idea that she'd have the nerve to pull the trigger . . ."

Miranda decided offense was the best tactic. "Exactly how long have you suspected her?" she asked, frowning. "Don't tell me that the authorities had her under surveillance since Passau."

"You're the darnedest woman I know for jumping at conclusions. And they're always the wrong ones."

"You must admit I'm consistent."

"Ummph." Mitch muttered something before taking another swallow of champagne. "Hadn't you better dry your hair?" he asked after surveying her.

"It's not very wet," Miranda assured him, running her fingers through it to check. She knew that she looked like a refugee from a locker room, but she wasn't going to flutter under his gaze just to win his approval. "I wish you'd stop changing the subject."

"You're confusing my motives. I just didn't want you to catch pneumonia because of me."

Her eyebrows rose. "I'm impressed. Don't worry. Temporary help can't claim any health benefits." She felt a surge of satisfaction as his fingers tightened on his glass, probably wishing it was her neck. A psychiatrist could really have a field day with them, she thought, blinking back the sudden tears that threatened to spill over. At least if she kept things on the flip side, Mitch would never know how he'd made confetti of her emotions during their brief time together.

He got to his feet and walked past her into the bathroom, emerging an instant later with a dry towel. "Here. Use it on your hair," he said, tossing it into her lap. And when she hesitated, he added in an ominously level tone, "If you don't, I'll do it for you."

"Oh, all right." She put her champagne on a shelf within reach and picked up the towel. "I'd still like to hear what's been going on," she muttered through its folds.

"That's a fair request," he said, lingering beside her for a moment until he went back to his place on the other divan. "You've been more than patient—at least that's what Marilyn said."

So he had already discussed her with his brunette. Miranda's lips came together and she murmured a few choice phrases into the towel.

"I beg your pardon?"

"Nothing important," Miranda snapped. "Did she decide exactly how much I could be told?"

Mitch's eyebrows came together. "You're off on another tangent! I knew it."

"Well, what do you expect?" Miranda threw down the damp towel in an angry gesture. "Good Lord, you treat me like a demented relative who's only able to understand words of one syllable. I'm surprised you haven't offered to cut up my meat at dinner."

He grinned, plainly amused by her anger. "I needn't have worried about your being back to normal. And *you* needn't worry about Marilyn—she's a charming lady. What did you say?"

"I just wondered why you're wasting your time talking to me."

"That wasn't what it sounded like," he informed her, "but it doesn't matter. We'll be meeting her for dinner when you finally get some clothes on. Marilyn and her husband," Mitch added as Miranda started to object. "I think you'll like them—they're old friends of mine."

"Her husband." Miranda's words were a bare thread of sound. "You didn't mention that she was married."

His lips quirked in a fleeting smile again. "Or that I was godfather to their son? I just hadn't gotten around to it. All of that would have been covered at Szentendre, if you hadn't staged such a hasty retreat."

"I thought Elsa needed some help," Miranda told him stiffly, trying to save a little bit of dignity. "She wasn't feeling well at the gallery."

"Was that another part of her act?" Mitch asked, turning the champagne glass with his lean fingers.

"Probably. Although the exhibit was awfully crowded and stuffy. That's why Janice almost collapsed. She's pregnant, though, so she was especially vulnerable."

Mitch's eyebrows climbed. "Lord, I didn't know that. Maybe I shouldn't have assigned them as your watchdogs."

"And that's another thing I'm mad about," Miranda said, sitting up straight. "What made you think I needed a couple of chaperons on a bus tour, for heaven's sake?"

"Because you'd bought a bud vase containing a film of some information that was supposed to stay hushed up."

"I'd done what?" Miranda's voice rose almost a full octave as she stared incredulously at him.

"Pipe down. Now you see why I didn't tell you before. You'd have given the game away for sure."

"I didn't even know we were playing one," she said faintly.

"To be honest, neither did I. At least until last night," Mitch admitted. "Then it occurred to me that there were too many questions without any answers. I remembered Marilyn and her husband at the embassy and decided to call them in to help. They were the ones who suspected a link to some information recently released by the War Crimes Commission."

"Real cloak-and-dagger stuff?" Miranda's voice became hushed as she thought about it. "Are you sure?"

"After that go-round with Elsa, I'm surprised that you need convincing."

"But why? Wait a minute—don't answer that until I come back." Miranda got up to toss the damp towel on a hook in the bathroom. She emerged with a hairbrush, attempting to create some order from the tangles as she stood in front of the dressing-table mirror. "Was it because of Joe? I mean, was Elsa trying to protect him?"

"Wrong generation. It's World War II information that's just been released." Mitch stood up to refill her glass and then topped his own after he sat down again. "And don't feel badly about misreading the clues—I never would have guessed without the embassy staff here turning up some background information on the Millers. Or, to be more specific, the Muellers. They anglicized the spelling of their name when they came to the U.S. after the war."

"Elsa and her husband?" Miranda tried to subdue a damp strand of hair before turning to look at him.

"But if there'd been any suspicion, they couldn't have gotten in, could they?"

"Go to the head of the class," Mitch said, raising his glass in mock salute. "According to the records at the time, they were squeaky clean, and after a few years, when her husband started piling up millions in land and oil deals—their German roots were carefully buried under a thick Southern accent."

"Her husband is dead, isn't he?" Miranda asked, wrinkling her forehead as she tried to remember what she'd been told.

Mitch nodded.

"Then why all the fuss now?" Miranda put down her brush and leaned against the dressing table. "Surely the Immigration Service wouldn't—" As he started to shake his head, she began again, "Anyhow, Joe is a U.S. citizen, isn't he? He certainly sounds like one with his Southern accent. Although Elsa's is almost as natural as Joe's."

"Apparently she took care of all the stray ends over the years and evidently thought she could relax. It must have been an awful shock when some of her old acquaintances latched on to some evidence in connection with the War Crimes report—evidence worth lots of money to suppress."

Miranda's eyebrows climbed as she took in the substance of his remark. "Wait a minute—you mean that Elsa is the one who was incriminated? That she was being blackmailed?" Miranda considered the accusation and then said forcefully, "You must be mistaken. I could see Elsa fighting to protect her family, but not anything else."

"You're not all wrong. Elsa undoubtedly had Joe's inheritance in mind, but I can't think she would have gone on paying blackmail forever to keep her reputation intact. She wanted to get hold of the original of that document, and this cruise was a perfect way to appear in the neighborhood. After that, she could make contact with the blackmailers and try to get off the hook permanently—anything to destroy the evidence." Before Miranda could ask, he said simply, "The document they had showed that Elsa was a German Army nurse during World War II."

"For Pete's sake, what's so incriminating about that?"

Mitch's voice hardened. "Elsa was assigned to a unit with a very unsavory reputation. Saving lives wasn't the main item on their agenda. The witnesses who survived testified that there was medical experimentation that doesn't bear repeating."

"Good God!"

He nodded, his expression grim. "According to what our embassy could dig up in a fast search, there's no actual evidence that Elsa did more than follow orders, but it's like the old saying—if you wallow in the pigsty . . ."

". . . you come out plastered with mud," Miranda finished for him. "I can see why Elsa'd do most anything to hush it up." She absently rubbed a finger down the side of her glass. "But she must have known that I wasn't threatening her."

"Look at it from her side of the coin. You book passage on the same cruise—share the same table at lunch—and later I point out that you're an aspiring journalist. Probably you even announced that you'd done considerable research on this part of the world before the trip. It could all fit. You could have been put on board to keep an eye on the two of them." Mitch took a final swallow of champagne and deposited the glass on a table at his elbow. "That's why I imagine they gave you a warning at Durnstein."

"On the stairs?" Miranda's eyes widened in surprise. "You think they were involved in that?"

"I'd put money on it. It might take some time to get Joe to admit his part, but he's already trying to see what kind of a deal he can make with the authorities—or so Marilyn reported."

"It will have to be Joe," Miranda agreed. "Elsa isn't going to confess anything. There's pure steel in her backbone."

"I know. That's why it's fortunate that we have the evidence on the film. Without that, there wouldn't be a chance of conviction. Elsa will hire the best defense lawyer money can buy."

Miranda nodded, her thoughts still on her harrowing experience at Durnstein. "I suppose they paid off somebody to do the actual dirty work on the stairs."

"Undoubtedly. But they were both ashore to check on the results. I'd guess they just wanted to discourage you and get you away from the scene—preferably by arranging a quick trip back to Munich, where you could nurse your skinned knees in comfort."

"They probably decided that you'd be only too happy to cooperate in that maneuver," Miranda agreed wryly. "Since you weren't enthusiastic about hiring me in the first place."

"You knew it and I knew it, but Joe and Elsa weren't aware of that angle." His crooked smile showed just for an instant. "If there's any infighting, I believe in doing it behind closed doors."

"Thanks very much."

"Not at all. Now, do you want to hear the rest of the story or sulk about that here in your cabin until dinner?"

"Dammit all! You are the most . . ." Desperately she searched for an adjective horrible enough to wipe that calm, assured expression off his face.

". . . genuine, certificated, honest-to-God bastard you've ever met?" he supplied helpfully.

"That'll do for a start." Her lips clamped together in annoyance as she stared angrily at him across the room. Then she shrugged, defeated again. "Never mind. Go on with the rest of the story."

"Saved by the bell," he said lightly. "Where was I?"

"Wishing you could toss me overboard in Durnstein."

"I thought you weren't going to sulk. And if you throw that glass at me, I'll turn you over my knee—bruises and all," he warned, as she hefted her empty champagne glass. There was a long moment of silence before Miranda carefully replaced the glass. He settled back again to say, "I wasn't happy with the goings-on, but I thought I could keep an eye on you so that they wouldn't be repeated. Your planned nightclub date with Joe made me a little uneasy, and after Frieda's accident the red flag went up for sure."

"He wasn't to blame for that, was he?"

Mitch shook his head. "It was the devastation I saw in her cabin. That bud vase she'd bought had been smashed and ground into the carpet. Some of her other belongings were literally torn apart. It was more than a search—it was malicious vandalism with sadistic overtones. The real danger didn't sink in until you dragged an identical vase out of your purse. Combined with Joe's hasty exit with Stefan after the nightclub visit, a pattern started to emerge. Gerhard promised to keep an eye on your cabin for the rest of the night, and when I found that I couldn't get back from the embassy this morning in time to join the tour, I recruited Farrell and Janice as watchdogs. Unfortunately, I couldn't say anything at that point, so they didn't know how important it was to stick close."

"It wasn't their fault that they didn't. I promised to meet them at the square, but Elsa made me change my plans."

"Dear Elsa," Mitch said ruefully, "whom we all underestimated. She played that sweet, frail little-old-lady role to perfection. After seeing that film the blackmailers had sent to her in the vase . . ."

"You've never told me what was on it," Miranda complained.

"It was a list of names on an old military ledger sheet identifying her as a supervisory nurse in that horror outfit. Even then, the embassy people thought there might be some mistake. That's why Marilyn came along for official reconnoitering at Szentendre."

"Let's go back a little so I can get things straight— you mean that salesgirl at the corner shop let me buy the wrong vase?"

"That's right. Joe was supposed to pick it up and dispose of the film as an extra safeguard. Apparently the blackmailers proclaimed it was evidence of their good faith. Once Elsa met their demands for a final payment, they'd keep her secret forever." Mitch's tone turned sarcastic. "Or at least until the next payment."

"But Elsa couldn't allow any suspicion in the meantime," Miranda deduced. "That's what she meant about her big gamble. There must have been millions involved."

"Cheap at half the price," Mitch said. "There's no going back now after the authorities identified her with that ledger sheet. War crimes don't lessen through the passage of years. It was just damned lucky that I caught a glimpse of you getting into that car with her at Szentendre."

Color rose under Miranda's cheekbones as she remembered how well she'd cooperated with Elsa in that maneuver. After seeing Mitch and Marilyn, she would have thumbed a ride with Jack the Ripper if it would have ensured a quick trip out of town.

"You made good time getting back to Budapest," she said, hoping that he'd take her lead and change the subject.

"Not as good as Stefan," he said grimly. "He was proud of that."

"Then you found him, after all?"

"Oh, yes. He was still in the car. When the police took charge of him, he started protesting his innocence. Claims he didn't know anything about blackmail—his only job was to act as chauffeur."

"It might be true."

"Who knows? I, for one, don't care." Mitch checked his watch and then got to his feet. "I'm bowing out and so are you—after you give the authorities a statement on being held at gunpoint by Elsa. That's one testimony that her defense attorney is going to have trouble surmounting."

"I'll be glad to cooperate," Miranda began, only to have him cut in impatiently.

"That can wait until tomorrow. You're in no condition for any more official business tonight."

"Hey, wait a minute!" Her protest stopped him midway to the stateroom door. "You're giving me orders again."

"It's about time somebody did," he said, raking his glance over her as he lingered by the dressing table. "I'll go check with Gerhard about a good place for dinner—God knows we don't want to hit another place like that nightclub. There must be someplace that plays Hungarian music instead of—" His words stopped as he noticed the piece of stationery that she'd left on the dressing table when he'd first arrived. Mitch picked it up gingerly, as if it should be marked with a skull and crossbones. "What the bloody hell is this?"

"Just what it looks like," Miranda told him, trying to sound calm about throwing away her future. "A letter of resignation. My letter of resignation," she added, in case there was any doubt.

"Christ! I should have known," he told her, disgust in every syllable. "That's the only maneuver you've missed on the whole cruise. I'm just surprised that you've waited this long." His glance went back to the paper and then he pursed his lips thoughtfully as he read it again. "On the other hand," he said when he'd finished, "maybe it's for the best."

Miranda had heard about people's hearts slipping down to their boots and always thought it was an absurd literary allusion. At Mitch's comment, however, all of her insides—everything that made her tick—slithered down to her heels and stayed there. She swallowed with difficulty, managing to say, "I'll get my things together and try to arrange a flight home. I'm not sure what to do about the article."

"Oh, that." He waved a dismissing hand. "Forget about it. We have plenty of backup stuff that can be used. And there's no need to leave the cruise. I just thought we might enjoy it from now on."

She stared at him dazedly. "I don't understand. Why on earth should I stay around? I gathered you couldn't wait to get rid of me."

Mitch moved his feet restlessly. He fingered his

shirt collar as if it had suddenly gotten too tight, and then just as rapidly dropped his hand to his side again when he saw Miranda's eyebrows climb in sudden suspicion. "Maybe," she said slowly, "you'd better tell me exactly what's going on."

"My God, you mean you don't know?" A whimsical expression washed over his features for a fleeting second. "I thought I'd made a complete idiot of myself from the very beginning."

"At the very beginning, the only thing you made clear was that hiring me was a distinct mistake," she mocked. Then as she saw his shoulders start to shake in silent laughter, she went on doggedly, "And if you're honest, you'll admit it."

He leaned against the top of the dressing table and rubbed the back of his neck while considering her accusation. "Okay, I'll plead guilty. I realized from my first glance that you were going to be trouble. And if *you're* honest, you'll admit that I was right about that."

"That isn't fair. How could I know that the Millers were still fighting World War II? I don't normally go around with people who push me down stairs or stick a gun in my side."

"And I don't normally go around putting aspiring female journalists to bed," Mitch assured her. When he saw her sudden frown, he added, "No matter what the tabloids report."

"I never did thank you for that," Miranda said, deciding that she'd better be truthful.

"You'll have to admit I was a perfect gentleman at the time," he pointed out, as color flooded her cheeks. "I even surprised myself."

"You could have called in a stewardess."

"It was enough of a miracle that I didn't decide to

share your bed." A wry expression softened his stern features. "As it was, I considered shopping around for a halo."

She pretended to be severe, although it was hard over the thumping of her heart. "You still have a way to go before you corner the market on those."

"Maybe, but I wouldn't bet on it. It's sobering to realize what you've accomplished in a few days," he added in a wondering tone.

Under such blatant flattery, it was hard for Miranda to keep her head. At that moment, she just longed for Mitch to ignore the safe distance between them and sweep her into his arms. Only her conscience, which was fighting a losing battle to stay alive, made her say unevenly, "I think I liked it better when you were shouting at me. This way, I don't stand a chance."

"Good." He crossed his arms over his chest with a deliberate gesture, as if determined to stay out of trouble. "That's what I hoped for all along. Now what's the matter?" he asked, a frown marring his expression as he saw her shake her head.

"I'm sorry, but I can't handle an affair with you," Miranda said unhappily, knowing she was turning her back on paradise as she spoke. She hitched her robe tighter around her, not realizing that the move outlined her figure even more faithfully. As Mitch's brooding glance slid over her, warmth suffused her entire body—as if he'd reached out and caressed her. The illusion was so strong that she sounded almost desperate as she went on. "It's probably stupid and old-fashioned, but I'm just not equipped for a short-term relationship. This way, it's better—"

"Shut up!" he interrupted tersely.

"—in the long run . . ." Her voice blanked out as his command registered. "What did you say?"

"I said to shut up," he told her, his jaw tight with annoyance. "What in the hell makes you think I want a quick week with you before going on to greener pastures?"

She swallowed, trying for a coherent answer under his angry gaze. "Well—everybody's heard about your opinion of marriage. I knew about that before I left New York."

"And you decided to take a bunch of gossip columns as the gospel. All right, so maybe some of that reputation was deserved," he admitted as she stared unwaveringly back at him, "but it didn't take long for me to know that what I feel now is different. My God, one look at you in Munich and I could hardly utter a sane sentence. It was a wonder I even managed to put you on the right bus. After I finally got you on your way, I couldn't wait to phone Gerhard for an extra cruise passage." He shook his head, remembering. "I had to drive like a madman to beat you to the boat."

Miranda's eyes widened incredulously. "Honestly? It really happened?"

Mitch put up his palm in a mock-serious gesture. " 'Struth. Every word."

"But you didn't give any indication . . ." She drew a tremulous breath and started again. "You weren't even very nice—playing the heavy employer every chance you got."

"Well, I certainly wasn't going around wearing a black band." He grimaced wryly. "As a matter of fact, I was fighting back at that point. It wasn't until you were hurt at Durnstein that I threw in the towel. All I wanted then was to keep you safe and well—

even if I had to sit beside you all night. But after undressing you and putting you to bed, I decided it was wiser to get some distance between us." He shot her an irritated glance. "Like now. And it would certainly make things easier if you wore a few more clothes occasionally. After we're married, it'll be different, but until then you'd better change your ways."

"What did you say?" she interrupted him ruthlessly.

"I said to put some clothes on."

"Not that. The last part. Oh, you beast!" she said as she saw him start to grin. She surged to her feet and found, happily, that he had moved at the same time, pulling her into his arms in the middle of the stateroom.

He tipped her chin up so that she had to meet his gaze—a gaze so warm and loving that she wondered how she could ever have found it otherwise. "Make it fast, darling. The sooner we get out of this cabin— the safer it'll be," he warned.

"But you haven't even asked me—"

"—to get married? You're right. I'm telling you. All we have to do now is find out how fast it can be accomplished in Budapest. Marilyn promised to check it out at the embassy, so that's why I don't want to be late."

Miranda's heartbeat was pounding so hard in her ears that she could hardly hear him. "That's all very well, but you haven't said anything about . . ." Her voice faltered and then strengthened. "About love."

"Idiot." He dropped a fast but thorough kiss on her upturned lips. "There's all the love in the world and you damned well better believe it. I've been waiting all my life for you. Thank God, I had sense enough to know it. You know it too." Feeling her uneven, indrawn breath, he tightened his clasp. "Say it, Miranda."

She couldn't restrain a shudder of delight and she felt a trail of fire as his hands caressed her. "Of course, I love you." Her voice was a mere whisper until she saw his eyes darken at her response, and then her nervousness disappeared. "I've been suffering tortures at the thought of leaving you," she told him, touching his face with gentle fingers—relieved to confess her true feelings, at last.

"I have no intention of letting you out of my sight for the next fifty years or so." The feel of her soft body was obviously playing havoc with his resolve and he uttered a muffled groan, pulling her even tighter as he lowered his lips to hers.

The angle of sunlight behind the stateroom drapes had shifted considerably before Miranda recaptured enough of her senses to realize that they'd gravitated to the divan in the interval.

Mitch pulled himself reluctantly upright, but kept her close to him. "Dammit all, woman, I'm going to get that ring on your finger first if it kills me. And it might come down to that. Hey! Where are you going?"

"You're not the only one who can make sacrifices," she teased as she pulled her robe back to a semblance of respectability. "I'll go get dressed for dinner."

"Don't be so hasty," he said, putting out a detaining hand when she swung her feet to the carpet. "I believe in a policy of taking things in the proper order. For example, this comes next."

Miranda drew a surprised, ecstatic breath as he moved suddenly beside her. "That's *not* the way to ever get out of this stateroom," she warned, trying to sound severe when he straightened again a moment later.

"You're right," he admitted, gazing solemnly back at her. "However, I needed to mark the exact spot and not leave things to chance." He grinned then at her puzzled expression and dropped a quick kiss on the end of her nose. "I'm giving you fair warning, my dearest, darling Miranda—once I get the ring on your finger, I'm not wasting any more time."

About the Author

Glenna Finley is a native of Washington State. She earned her degree from Stanford University in Russian Studies and in Speech and Dramatic Arts, with emphasis on radio.

After a stint in radio and publicity work in Seattle, she went to New York City to work for NBC as a producer in its international division. In addition, she worked with the "March of Time" and *Life* magazine.

As a producer, she had her own show about activities in Manhattan, a show that was broadcast to England. The programs were similar to those of the "Voice of America."

Though her life in New York was exciting, she eventually returned to the Northwest where she married. She loves to travel, and draws heavily on her travels and experiences for the novels that have been published. Her books for NAL have sold several million copies.